AUG 1 8 2017

THE Sisters 8

BOOK 2

DURINDA'S DANGERS

By Lauren Baratz-Logsted
With Greg Logsted & Jackie Logsted

Illustrated by Lisa K. Weber

sandpiper

HOUGHTON MIFFLIN HARCOURT
BOSTON

For information about permission to reproduce selections
from this book, write to trade.permissions@hmhco.com or to
Permissions, Houghton Mifflin Harcourt Publishing Company,
3 Park Avenue, 19th Floor, New York, New York 10016.

www.hmhco.com

SANDPIPER and SANDPIPER logo are trademarks of
Houghton Mifflin Harcourt Publishing Company.

The text of this book is set in Youbee.
Book design by Carol Chu.

Library of Congress Cataloging-in-Publication Data

Baratz-Logsted, Lauren.
Durinda's dangers / by Lauren Baratz-Logsted ; with Greg
Logsted and Jackie Logsted.
p. cm. — (The sisters eight ; bk. 2)
Summary: One month after their parents' disappearance,
the third-grade Huit octuplets deal with a malfunctioning
refrigerator and try to win the love of the only boy in
their class at Valentine's Day, while Durinda discovers
her special power and gift.
ISBN 978-0-547-13347-8 (hardcover edition)
ISBN 978-0-547-05339-4 (pbk. edition)
[1. Sisters—Fiction. 2. Abandoned children—Fiction. 3.
Valentine's Day—Fiction. 4. Schools—Fiction. 5. Refrigerators—
Fiction.] I. Logsted, Greg. II. Logsted, Jackie. III. Title.
PZ7.B22966Dur 2008
[Fic]—dc22

2008013305

Printed in the United States of America
DOC 20 19 18 17 16 15 14 13 12 11
4500638921

For Merie Kirshner & Jackie's class
at the Wooster School

Thank you for so enthusiastically
listening to book one. We hope you enjoy
book two even more.

Annie   Durinda   Georgia   Jackie

Marcia   Petal   Rebecca   Zinnia

PROLOGUE

The story always begins the same . . . until it changes.

Once upon a time, there were eight sisters who would all one day be eight years old.

At the same time.

They were octuplets, you see.

Their names were Annie, Durinda, Georgia, Jackie, Marcia, Petal, Rebecca, and Zinnia. They were each born a minute apart on August 8, 2000. All eight had brown hair and brown eyes. And although they were all the same exact age, give or take a few minutes, each was one inch taller than the next, with Zinnia being the shortest and Annie the tallest.

On New Year's Eve 2007, their parents disappeared, or died. Their mother went into the kitchen for eggnog, their father went out to the woodshed for firewood, and neither returned.

Now the Eights must figure out what happened to their parents while keeping the outside world from discovering that eight little girls are home alone.

At the beginning of their first adventure, also known as *The Sisters Eight, Book 1: Annie's Adventures*, the girls became aware of the disappearance of their parents, and they found a note hidden behind a loose stone in the wall of the drawing room of their magnificent home. The note read:

Dear Annie, Durinda, Georgia, Jackie, Marcia, Petal, Rebecca, and Zinnia,

This may come as rather a shock to you, but it appears you each possess a power and a gift. The powers you already have—you merely don't know you have them yet. The gifts are from your parents, and these you must also discover for yourselves. In fact, you must each discover both your power and your gift in order to reveal what happened to your parents. Have you got all that?

The note was unsigned.

During the course of *Annie's Adventures,* Annie discovered her power: the ability to be as smart as an adult when needed. She also discovered her gift: a lovely ring with a purple gemstone in it.

And what *did* happen to their parents? Well, we don't know that yet, do we? If we did, then this would be the end of our story, not the continuation . . .

CHAPTER ONE

It was the first week in February, and it wasn't like our lives were getting any easier.

Our parents, having disappeared on New Year's Eve when Mommy went to the kitchen to get eggnog and Daddy went out to the woodshed for more firewood, were still missing. Or dead.

We still hadn't found a way to get into the home of our evil neighbor the Wicket so we could find out what she had stolen from Mommy's Top Secret folder.

And we were still in the third grade at the Whistle Stop, a private school running from kindergarten through twelfth grade, where we were forced to wear ugly yellow plaid uniforms.

We were at the Whistle Stop that morning. Our only classmates were Will Simms, a towheaded boy we liked, and Mandy Stenko, a redheaded girl we didn't. Our teacher, Mrs. McGillicuddy, known to us Eights as the McG, was going on and on about something.

The McG was a tall blonde with a long nose, on the bridge of which perched horn-rimmed glasses. On this particular morning, the thing she was going on and on about was hearts.

"The heart," the McG said, "is the organ that pumps blood through your body."

"I'm pretty sure we knew that already," Georgia said.

"Is there going to be a test on this?" Petal wanted to know.

The McG ignored us.

"The heart," the McG went on, "is also one of four symbols on playing cards, the other three being the club, the diamond, and the spade."

"Does this have anything to do with your giving Will soccer trading cards for his birthday last month?" Durinda asked.

"Will doesn't even like soccer," Rebecca pointed out, forgetting how Annie had encouraged us to pretend he did on the day the McG had given Will the cards.

The McG glared at us.

"Sorry," Jackie said with a peacemaking shrug. "We thought you'd want to know."

The McG ignored us some more.

"There are several holidays in the month of February," the McG went on. "Some are national, like

Presidents' Day; one has to do with predicting the weather for the next six weeks; and the third is of a far more important nature. Does anyone know the most important holiday in February?"

"Groundhog Day?" Marcia suggested. Then she observed, "It should be. The weather is very important to farmers, not that we know any farmers."

"Do we get presents on Groundhog Day?" Zinnia asked, her eyes lighting up.

We could be wrong about this, but we were pretty certain the McG was getting frustrated with us.

"No, of course it's not Groundhog Day!" the McG practically shouted. "How could it—?" She shook her head, as though refusing to travel down a particular conversational road with us for fear of what it might do to her brain. She forced a sweet smile. "Anyone else have any ideas?"

Mandy Stenko raised her hand eagerly. You'd think she had to go to the bathroom or something.

That was Mandy all over. The rest of us never bothered raising our hands before saying what was on our minds.

Mandy squirmed in her chair until we all started thinking she really *did* have to go to the bathroom. But the McG finally called on her and Mandy stopped squirming.

"Yes, Mandy?"

"Valentine's Day!" Mandy burst out. And once the cork had been taken out of the Mandy bottle, there was no stopping her. "Valentine's Day," she continued breathlessly, "is the holiday that occurs each year on February fourteenth. My mother says it's a day when people should give other people flowers or candy or gifts. My father says it was invented by the greeting-card companies and that it is a poor trick to play on husbands who shouldn't be expected to know the exact right gift without someone telling them first."

"That's a rather . . . *novel* interpretation," the McG said. "But you left out one important thing in your recitation."

Mandy looked at the McG, puzzled.

Okay, we'll admit it: we were all puzzled.

"You left out *romance*," the McG said, a wistful expression overtaking her usually stern face. "You left out *love*."

What was the McG talking about?

Romance?

Love?

Had Principal Freud's forcing her to be our teacher since last September caused the McG to lose whatever was left of her tiny little mind?

"The heart of something," the McG said, "can be said to be the center of that thing. And the heart itself, that organ that beats in your chest at the average rate of seventy-two beats per minute, can be said to be the center of love." She removed her glasses. Then she wiped a tear from her eye, replaced her glasses on her nose, and went on. "When you give your red folders to your parents this week, be sure they look at them very carefully."

Every Tuesday, red folders containing Important Papers were sent home. It was Annie's job, since it was her power to be as smart as an adult when she had to be, to go through the red folders. Now that our parents were gone, she made sure that everything was done as it should be and nothing aroused the suspicions of the People in Authority.

We may not have had parents anymore, at least not anywhere we could see them, but we did have Annie.

We were confident Annie would never make a mistake that would land us in the stew.

"This week's red folders," the McG went on, which we

thought was silly since she'd just told us to have our parents look at them very carefully, "will contain special information about our upcoming celebration of Valentine's Day, the holiday of love. It is critical that all instructions be followed to a T."

"Why do people always say 'to a T'?" Will asked.

Eight heads, ours, swiveled to look at Will.

"I mean," Will went on, amiable as always, "I don't want to be difficult, but why isn't the phrase 'to an A'? Or 'to a D' or 'to a G' or 'to a J' or 'to an M' or 'to a P' or 'to an R' or 'to a Z'? It just seems to me that every time one of you educators or parents uses that 'to a T' phrase, you run the risk of making all the other letters in the alphabet feel bad."

We suppose we should have paid more attention to the McG's Special Instructions Regarding Valentine's Day.

We definitely should have read the contents of the folder more carefully. The two-sheet printout, stapled together at the top, said: "Valentines: You will need to make or buy one for each of the following classmates so that it will be *fair* and *everyone* will have a *good* time. Please keep this handy checklist with you when you do your shopping and fill out your valentines because it is *critical* that *no one* feel *left out* (but of course don't make one for yourself because that would

be silly, also it would look like you perhaps like yourself a bit too much):

> Annie Huit
> Durinda Huit
> Georgia Huit
> Jackie Huit
> Marcia Huit
> Petal Huit
> Rebecca Huit
> Zinnia Huit
> Will Simms
> Mandy Stenko

P.S. For valentine-making purposes, your teacher's name
is spelled *Mrs. McGillicuddy.*"

We blame Annie for what happened later. It was her
job to see that all the Important Papers in the Tuesday
red folders got read. Or perhaps we should blame the
school secretary, for double-spacing between our names
when single-spacing would have worked just fine—we
are not, after all, stupid—meaning that the last few lines
ran onto a second page, which we never saw.

Or maybe the real culprit was Love.

For during Will's speech about how people shouldn't

favor the letter *T* and leave other letters out of things, eight hearts had gone *sproing!* in eight chests, and our eyes had filled with something as we looked at him.

And that something was love.

* * * * * * * *

It was on the long bus ride home that we came up with our plan.

We didn't love riding the school bus. What we used to love was having Mommy drive us to school in the great big purple Hummer that she, being a scientist and also an outstanding inventor, had doctored so it was an environmentally sound vehicle. But Mommy was no longer around, and even though Annie had tricked Pete the mechanic into teaching her how to drive, she couldn't drive us to school every day, not even if she wore her Daddy disguise that she wore from time to time, because if she did then the People in Authority might catch on.

And that would be very bad.

But not everything in our lives was very bad, because now we were hatching a plan.

"I'm going to make Will the best valentine he's ever seen," Durinda announced.

"No, I am," said Annie.

"No, I am," said Georgia.

"No, I am," said Jackie.

"No, I am," said Marcia.

"No, I am," said Petal.

"No, I am," said Rebecca.

"No, I am," said Zinnia. Then she added, "Do you think he'll give us stupendous presents in return?"

We all glared at one another.

"Speaking of presents," Jackie suggested, "in addition to making valentines for Will, perhaps we should each buy him a special present too?"

But Durinda pointed out that Annie was the only one of us who knew how to use the checkbook and credit cards and forge Daddy's name in order to get money to pay for things.

"It wouldn't be fair," Durinda said. "Annie might only give each of us, say, five dollars to spend, while allowing herself far more. And how would we ever know?"

We all glared at Annie.

"No," Durinda said, "for this to be fair, we need to limit ourselves to each using her talents to create the best possible valentine for Will."

So that was our plan.

We were going to have a competition to see who could make the best valentine for Will.

So we could discover which one of us he loved best.

Once and for all.

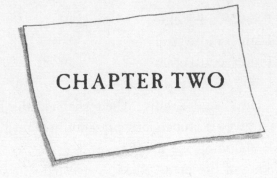

CHAPTER TWO

We arrived home expecting to start on our valentines for Will right away.

What we hadn't planned on was arriving home to disaster.

"There's something wrong with the talking refrigerator!" Durinda called out to us from the kitchen, where she had gone with Jackie to make us a snack. Since Mommy had disappeared, it was Durinda's job to prepare our food.

We all raced in to see what she was talking about.

"Those look like drops of some sort of clear liquid. They've made a puddle on the floor in front of the talking refrigerator," Marcia observed. "There are so many of them!"

The talking refrigerator was one of Mommy's inventions. It told us when we were getting low on necessary food items, or even luxury food items, and it always encouraged us to eat more.

Durinda crouched in front of the talking refrigerator. Then she put one of her fingers into the puddle and raised that finger toward her tongue.

"Don't do it!" Zinnia shouted.

"It could have been left there by the ax murderer!" Petal shouted.

"Are you crazy?" Georgia wondered.

"It's her funeral." Rebecca harrumphed.

But it didn't matter what any of us shouted, wondered, or harrumphed, for Durinda at last touched her finger to her tongue. Then she tilted her head back, thinking.

"Tears," she decided at last. "These drops are salty. They taste like tears."

"Salty could be good right around now," Annie said. "I rather fancy a salty snack, if you could come up with a healthy one."

"Well, let's see what we've got," Durinda said, pulling open the door.

But when the door was fully opened, rather than seeing the lovely array of food we were accustomed to, we saw . . .

"Eek!" Durinda shouted. "Everything is melting!"

It was true.

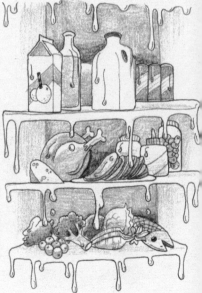

All our food had little droplets of water on it, like you get when you take a cold peach from the crisper and put it somewhere warmer, like the counter.

And we smelled something foul right away too: the milk was starting to spoil.

"What is going on?"

Durinda demanded. "And why isn't the refrigerator talking to us?"

She had a point.

Usually, by this time, the refrigerator would have said lots of things to us. But now? Nothing.

The talking refrigerator had gone silent.

Then we noticed more liquid dripping from the top freezer, and Durinda yanked open that door.

The freezer was melting.

And it wasn't *just* melting. When Durinda opened the door, a river of melted ice came flooding out at us.

We eight stood there, soaked, too shocked to say anything.

Even Georgia and Rebecca were shut up by this.

And then, into our stunned silence, entered a sound.

It was the sound of someone—or some*thing*—sobbing.

"I'm me-e-e-elting!" the talking refrigerator gasped out between sobs.

"What do you think is wrong with it?" Jackie asked, concerned.

"I'm not sure," Marcia said, "but it sounds depressed."

"What's wrong?" Durinda asked the talking refrigerator directly.

Since the kitchen was Durinda's province, the rest of us were content to let her take over the refrigeration interrogation.

"Carl is heartbroken!" the talking refrigerator said.

"Who is Carl?" Durinda asked, perplexed.

"Carl is . . . is . . . *me!*" the talking refrigerator cried.

We all looked at one another: *Carl?*

"Carl?" Jackie voiced all of our thoughts. "But I always thought the talking refrigerator was a girl!"

It was true. We had all thought that.

We shrugged our shoulders. Who knew?

"And why is, er, *Carl* heartbroken?" Durinda asked in a soothing tone.

"Because Carl is in love with Betty . . . *and Betty never even seems to notice Carl!*"

Betty, like Carl, was one of our mother's inventions. She was a black and gold robot who was supposed to make our life easier by cleaning, but Betty seemed to have gotten her job description all wrong.

As though to illustrate this, Betty came rolling through the room, used her pincer hands to throw a bag of dust rags in the air like so much confetti, and then rolled back out again.

And as though to prove Carl's point, she completely disregarded Carl when he shouted after her, "*Bet-ty!*" like some T-shirt-wearing maniac in the rain outside a building in the South or something.

"There, there, Carl," Durinda soothed, looking for

the proper place to pat Carl. "It'll be all right."

"No, it won't!" Carl said. "Valentine's Day is coming! I don't even want to *live,* and I don't see how I can properly concentrate on keeping food cold if I can't have Betty!"

Apparently, the prospect of Valentine's Day had the whole world going bonkers.

"There, there," Durinda said again. "It'll all work out."

"But how?" Georgia demanded.

"We'll all starve!" Petal said. "First we became orphans, and now we're going to be starving orphans!"

"I'll bet Carl could win Betty's heart," Zinnia said, "if he bought her a really great present."

"I wonder if a new refrigerator is in our budget?" Annie wondered. "Perhaps I should just go look at the checkbook—"

"Don't. You. Dare." It was amazing to hear Durinda speak so harshly to Annie, but we supposed that having the talking refrigerator melt from love before your very eyes when your domain is the kitchen could be disturbing. "It'll all work out. No one will starve. Now, everyone except Jackie, shoo. I've got to figure out what to make for dinner, since we've wasted so much of the afternoon on love that snack time is long gone."

* * * * * * * *

While Durinda and Jackie set about finding something to make for dinner that did not require foods that had been properly refrigerated, the rest of us set to work making valentines for Will. Durinda and Jackie would get their crack at the art supplies after they served us dinner.

We gathered together all the craft supplies we could find: construction paper, scissors, markers, glitter, feathers, sequins, paste. Of those items, Georgia loved the paste best; Rebecca loved the scissors—which she liked to run with—while Petal and Zinnia fought continually over the glitter, feathers, and sequins. Marcia was happy as long as she had a little bit of everything, and Annie was happy if we didn't kill one another and left her in peace.

You might think it strange that we could devote so much time to worrying about valentine competitions and the love life of a talking refrigerator when our parents were missing. Or dead. But you must realize: (1) our parents had been missing for more than a month; (2) we had no idea where to look for them; (3) it took much of our energy each day merely to survive—get the grocery shopping done, keep ourselves and our eight cats fed and cleaned, learn how to drive cars and pay bills, all while keeping the outside adult world from realizing that there were eight kids home alone; and so (4) it was impossible to remain sad and worried every second of the day.

So we cut, colored, glittered, and pasted little bits of feathers and sequins all over one another until it was time for Durinda to call us in to dinner.

After all our handy-dandy artwork, we were positively famished. Before dinner, we collected Daddy Sparky and Mommy Sally from the drawing room and set them up in the dining area. Daddy Sparky was a suit of armor. Mommy Sally was a dressmaker's dummy. Not long after Mommy and Daddy disappeared, or died, we dressed Sparky and Sally as our parents so that if nosy neighbors like the Wicket peeked in, they would think our parents were home. At mealtimes now, we liked to keep them in the room with us. It felt like having real parents, except they couldn't talk, which was sometimes a good feature for a parent to have.

As we settled at our places around the dining room table, after following Annie's instructions to wash our hands first, we were anticipating a satisfying meal. Perhaps it would be spaghetti and meatballs? Or maybe something truly spectacular, like that Thanksgiving-style dinner Durinda and Jackie threw together once for a celebration? It was all we could do to keep from rubbing our hands together in glee and salivating like dogs as Jackie held open the swinging doors for Durinda and Durinda entered with a silver platter piled high with . . .

"Peanut butter and jelly sandwiches?" Georgia fishwifed as Durinda set the platter down in the middle of the table. "You expect us to eat *that?* For *dinner?"*

"I think I'm feeling a nut allergy coming on," Petal said worriedly.

"You don't have nut allergies," Annie pointed out.

"This is wretched," Rebecca said, picking up one of the sandwiches and then throwing it down again in disgust. "What were you two doing in the kitchen all this time? It doesn't take that long to make wretched sandwiches."

Jackie blushed. "We were working on sketching out plans for our own Valentine's Day cards for Will. We didn't want to fall behind."

"Do you have any idea," Durinda said, "how hard it is to keep this family fed every day? How much energy it takes? And do you have any idea how hard it is to find something to prepare that is safe and nutritious but doesn't require refrigeration? You're all just lucky I don't quit."

Durinda was so angry, she was tapping her hand against her leg.

"We'll all really starve!" Petal said, not noticing

how angry Durinda was getting. "It will be awful! They will find our skinny bodies in the gutter!"

Later, we would think we all should have paid more attention to how angry Durinda was.

"The kid may be whiny," Georgia said of Petal, "but she does make a good point. We'll starve if we have to eat PBJs at every meal."

"We do get hot lunches at school," Annie pointed out.

"Doesn't matter," Georgia said. "It'll still be PBJs twice a day on weekdays and every meal on weekends."

"I'll go on a hunger strike," Rebecca threatened. "We all will. It's inhuman to give us—"

And that's when it happened.

Durinda, in her anger, patted her right hand against her leg three times, then pointed sharply at Georgia as though her finger were a gun. "You. Shut. Up."

Who knew Durinda had so much anger in her?

Perhaps it was because she had to cook for us all the time.

Then Durinda turned slightly and did the same to Rebecca. Three leg pats, sharp point: "You. Shut. Up."

And Georgia and Rebecca froze right where they sat in their chairs, both with their mouths open as though they had been about to say something, probably something awful, and now couldn't.

They couldn't because they were frozen solid.

Like statues.

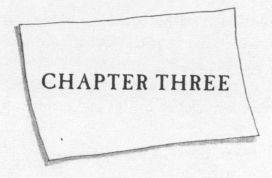

CHAPTER THREE

"Cut it out!" Durinda yelled at Georgia and Rebecca.

But they didn't cut it out.

Jackie crossed to where Georgia and Rebecca sat. Then she waved her hand in front of first Georgia's and then Rebecca's eyes.

Georgia and Rebecca remained frozen in position, their eyes glazed over as if seeing nothing.

Jackie leaned in, her lips close to Georgia's ear. *"Boo!"* she shouted as loud as she could.

Georgia didn't flinch.

Jackie turned to Rebecca, placed her lips close to Rebecca's ear, and said in a sweet voice, "We have a whole can of pink frosting just for you and you can eat it now before dinner."

Rebecca didn't salivate.

"Huh," Marcia observed, "they really are frozen like that. I wonder how long they'll remain this way?"

Petal looked at Durinda, real fear in her eyes. "What are you, some kind of witch? What have you done to Georgia and Rebecca?"

Without thinking, Durinda tapped her right hand three times fast against her leg and pointed sharply at Petal.

Petal froze where she sat, the look of horror unchanged on her face.

"Oh, my," Zinnia said in an awestruck voice. "I think you just found your power, and it's a doozy."

"I would have thought," Marcia said thoughtfully, "that you were using magic words, and those words were, 'You. Shut. Up.' But you didn't say any words to Petal at all just now and yet you froze her where she sat. I think it must be those three taps you give your leg combined with that sharp point of your finger."

"I wonder which power is better," Jackie wondered, "Annie's ability to be as smart as an adult or Durinda's to freeze people whenever she wants to."

"Oh, I'd say Durinda's," Zinnia said, a wistful expression on her face now. "I'd love to have a power like that."

Annie looked offended at this.

"But I didn't want to freeze anybody," Durinda objected. Now it was her turn to look horrified at what she'd done. "I just got angry and then it happened. I don't want this power! It's too much! It's too much . . . *power!*"

"Why don't we go check the loose stone in the drawing room?" Annie suggested reasonably.

It was a great idea, but we also suspected that Annie was trying to regain the center of power. After all she'd done for us, it probably didn't make her feel too good to think that we preferred Durinda's power to hers. And in truth, looking at the frozen bodies of Georgia, Rebecca, and Petal, we believed that Georgia, Rebecca, and Petal did not find Durinda's power as wonderful as we did.

We headed off to the loose stone in the drawing room. It was behind the loose stone that we'd found the first note, on New Year's Eve, announcing our parents' disappearance. And additional notes had appeared there after Annie had discovered her own power and gift.

Sure enough, behind the loose stone there was a new note.

Dear Durinda,

Nice work. Three down, thirteen to go.

As always, the note was unsigned.

"Whoever is leaving these notes," Marcia commented, "at least he or she has solid math skills."

"Well, that was easy," Jackie said.

"How do you mean?" Annie asked.

"It just seems to me," Jackie answered, "that it took you a long time to discover your power. But Durinda found hers right away."

"Does anyone else sense a pattern here?" Marcia asked.

"How do you mean?" Annie asked again.

"Well," Marcia answered, "first you found your power and gift, now Durinda has her power. There seems to be a clear pattern of discovery running from oldest to youngest."

Zinnia sighed a heavy sigh and collapsed into an overstuffed chair in front of the fireplace, her cheek sagging against her open palm. "That must mean I will discover my power last." A heavier sigh. "That's me all over: always the last at everything."

"But I don't want this power!" Durinda said. These were the first words she'd spoken since we'd entered the drawing room and found the new note. "It's too much! What if Georgia, Rebecca, and Petal remain frozen forever?"

Annie shrugged. "Would that really be so awful?" She thought about this. "Well, I suppose it would be sad if Petal never came back, but it is nice getting a break from all of her worrying."

"But I don't want them to be frozen forever!" Durinda objected. "Not any of them! It's fine to have Daddy Sparky and Mommy Sally be that way. One's a suit of armor and the other's a dressmaker's dummy. But not my own sisters!"

"Why don't we go back and check on them?" Annie suggested in a soothing voice.

So that's what we did.

Back in the dining room, Georgia, Rebecca, and Petal were right where we left them.

But then a minute later, just as it looked like Durinda was going to go all hysterical panicky again, Rebecca's eyelids fluttered, and she said, "PBJs for dinner after we've been slaving all day." It was as though Durinda hadn't frozen her after "It's inhuman to give us—"

It was obvious that wherever Rebecca had gone when she was frozen, she had no memory of it, if she'd even been anywhere at all other than empty space.

A moment later, Petal was back. Five minutes later, Georgia was with us too. None of us could figure out why it took Georgia the longest to come back, since she'd been frozen only a few seconds after Rebecca, but we accepted that there were some things in life for which there was no explanation. There were already so many things in our lives lacking explanations. What was one more?

It took us the longest time to persuade Georgia, Rebecca, and Petal that they'd been frozen, and then to convince Petal that Durinda wasn't a witch. In fact, we had to have Durinda freeze Marcia, which took much persuading—not of Marcia, who was happy to be the guinea pig, but to get Durinda to use her awesome power again—just to demonstrate.

Once Marcia was frozen, a thought occurred to Jackie. "How long did the others remain frozen before?"

It was a good question, to which none of us knew the answer.

Had it been ten minutes? Twenty? An hour? The first seemed too short, the last too long. But who knew what was going on with simple things that a person could usually depend on, like time, in our house?

"Get the stopwatch," Annie directed Zinnia.

Zinnia was the one of us Annie least liked to order around, but we suspected she did this now to make Zinnia feel better, like she had something important to do. It was obvious Zinnia still felt bad about learning that she would in all probability be the last one among us to receive her power and her gift.

"What's the stopwatch for?" Jackie asked when Zinnia returned with it.

"We're going to do time trials," Annie announced. "Durinda will freeze one of us and we'll use the timer to see how long it takes that person to become unfrozen again."

"But I'm not sure I want to—" Durinda began to object.

"Just do it!" Annie shouted at her.

Whatever else was going to happen tonight, one thing was certain: Annie would retain her position as acting head of the household in our parents' absence. Or death.

But once Durinda had agreed to the inevitable, she had no idea who she should freeze.

"I just don't know!" she said anxiously.

"Do me!" said Jackie.

"Do me!" said Zinnia.

"Do me again!" said Georgia.

"Do me again!" said Rebecca.

"Do me again!" said Petal.

Marcia probably would have said "Do me again!" too, but she was still frozen.

"I'd love to be frozen," Annie said, wearing a wistful expression on her face, perhaps at the thought of childhood lost, "but I have to run the stopwatch."

So that's what we did that night for the longest time: time trials, to see how long a person would remain frozen at Durinda's bidding.

As it turned out, how long a person remained frozen varied from person to person.

Georgia really was the longest. This time when Durinda froze her, she remained that way for nearly a whole hour. Petal was the shortest: just a scant seven minutes. We had no idea why Georgia was the most susceptible; she just was.

We even had Durinda freeze Annie after Annie had timed everyone else, and she lasted just a minute longer than Petal.

But there was a problem.

One of us wouldn't freeze.

"Why can't I freeze like everyone else?" Zinnia said, breaking into sobs. "This is just awful! First I learn I'll have to wait until after everyone else has gone to receive my power and my gift, and now I can't even be frozen like everyone else!"

"There, there," Annie said, putting her arm around Zinnia's trembling shoulders. "I'm not sure whether Marcia's right and you really will have to wait for everyone else before you receive your power and gift. But I do know one thing."

"What's that?" Zinnia asked.

"Not being able to be frozen?" Annie shrugged. "It means you're *special.* In a way, when you think about it, it's like you have a power all your own already: the power *not* to be frozen."

Zinnia's smile glittered through her tears.

"Why, look at Georgia," Annie went on. "The girl freezes at the drop of a hat. Now tell me, what's so special about that?"

Zinnia's smile glittered even brighter.

"That's right," Annie answered her own question. "There's nothing special about it at all."

We did all laugh at that. Lucky for us, Georgia was frozen yet again, staring into space like a zombie. If she hadn't been, there would no doubt have been the devil to pay.

Timidly, Zinnia approached Durinda. "That really is an awesome power you have there. I hope you use it wisely."

"Oh, it's just handy-dandy," Durinda scoffed. Durinda was still unsure of how she felt about all this.

"Oh, but it is," Zinnia said. "Why, between you and Annie, the two of you could probably take over the world."

"You know," Annie said to Durinda, "Zinnia is right. Your power will come in handy, once we figure out what best to use it for. In the meantime, it's kind of nice for me. I was getting lonely being the only one who had her power so far."

When everyone was unfrozen, we sat back down at the table.

And that night, after all that had happened, no one objected to eating the wretched PBJs for dinner.

CHAPTER FOUR

The next morning, we had boxed cereal for breakfast. It wasn't that we liked cold cereal, but when Durinda went to get the frozen pancakes out, she found a huge puddle in front of the freezer. Carl the talking refrigerator was still depressed that Betty the robot wouldn't return his affections.

"This really has to stop," Rebecca said, munching her dry cereal. All the milk had spoiled so there was no milk to put over it, and Marcia's suggestion to use water instead had gone over like a

lead balloon. "I'm a growing girl. I need proper hot meals."

"What do you have to complain about?" Durinda said, mop and bucket in hand. "I'm the one who has to clean up after Carl."

It was true. We'd tried to get Betty to do the cleanup, since it was her job, but she just went off to watch her morning cartoons.

"I think it's sad," Zinnia said. "Carl loves Betty so much. Why can't she just notice him a bit?"

"It's just like Romeo and Juliet." Petal heaved a romantic sigh. "Only Juliet is a robot who prefers watching *Dora the Explorer* to dying for love."

Unfortunately, Zinnia and Petal said these last two things within Carl's hearing, and he launched into a fresh river of tears.

"If this keeps up," Georgia said, leaping to avoid a new puddle, "we'll have to build an ark to get around our own home."

When we arrived at school, the McG had a notice written on the board: *Just 9 more shopping days left until Valentine's Day—don't forget to get all your cards!*

It was odd. This Valentine's Day stuff seemed so important to her. Was she going to keep this up—*8 more shopping days, 7 more shopping days, 6 more . . .*—until Valentine's Day was here?

Jackie pointed out, "Shouldn't we have celebrated Groundhog Day first?"

"A late celebration would be nice." Zinnia perked up. "You know: equal time for equal holidays and all of that."

The McG glared at us.

"Do you think," she said sternly, "that you can put a holiday where a rodent sees his shadow, or not, on an equal footing with one symbolized by Cupid and an arrow through the heart?"

Well, when she put it like that . . .

When we got home, we were determined to continue our competition to see who could make the best Valentine's Day card for Will. Annie had said that perhaps we each should work in a separate room so that no one could steal anyone else's ideas. Some of us thought this was taking paranoia over internal espionage too far, while others of us thought her idea was just peachy.

But before we could get down to making valentines, a new emergency arose.

"The cats are saying that Dandruff has been freezing them on and off all day," Zinnia said.

We had eight gray and white puffballs that were our cats, one for each sister. Their names were Anthrax, Dandruff, Greatorex, Jaguar, Minx, Precious,

Rambunctious, and Zither. Dandruff was Durinda's cat.

Zinnia always acted as though the cats talked to her, but we all knew that was a crazy idea.

So we ignored Zinnia and went to get our valentine supplies.

But five minutes into our card making, there was a shout heard round the house.

"Come quick!" Zinnia shouted. "There's something awful going on in Fall!"

We had four seasonal rooms in our home, which Mommy had created so we could go to the season we most wanted to be in when we grew tired of the one we were living in. The rooms were Winter, Spring, Summer, and Fall. Fall had orange and brown and red and yellow leaves painted all over the walls because Mommy said you couldn't manufacture leaves that crinkled properly in a lab.

We raced toward the sound of Zinnia's voice.

And what did we see?

Dandruff, in action.

Rambunctious and Greatorex were already frozen in position as we skidded into the room, but we were there to witness it when Precious, winded from running for what we guessed to be a long period of time, slowed down to gasp for breath. That's when we saw Dandruff lift her front right paw, tap it rapidly against her hind

leg three times, and then point it at Precious as though it were a loaded gun.

Precious froze where she stood.

Then we watched—some of us in horror, some of us amused—as Dandruff tracked down and froze Anthrax, Jaguar, and Minx. For some reason, Dandruff couldn't freeze Zither. But Zither was so frightened after what she'd seen Dandruff do to the others, she raced from the room and was not seen again for hours.

It made a very odd picture, all those frozen cats. It was as though six of our cats had decided to dress up as lawn jockeys for Halloween.

Then we watched as Dandruff casually sauntered out of the room, like a sheriff in a Western who has killed all the bad guys. We swear we heard her whistle a tune under her breath. Later, Marcia would tell us that tune was called "Rawhide."

Some of us may have been horrified, but we were also all curious, so we followed Dandruff out of the room to see what she would do next.

Dandruff made for the cat room. The cat room was like our drawing room, only for cats. It was where the cats all gathered when they wanted to be who they were or when they had something important to discuss. It was also where their eight kibble bowls were lined up, each bowl with the name of a different cat printed on it in pretty lettering. The names on the bowls had been Daddy's idea when he was still among us. Daddy was a great model—and by that we don't mean "an example," but rather "someone who looks great in designer clothes on the runways of Paris and Milan"—and he had a terrific artistic touch.

We watched as Dandruff moved through the bowls systematically, eating all the kibble in bowls marked *Anthrax* through *Zither.* She didn't stop until the last brown nugget of kibble was gone and her chops had been licked. Then she started grooming herself, cleaning her fur with her tongue as though she hadn't just done anything wrong or unusual.

"She's freezing the other cats," Durinda said of her own cat, "so she can eat what is rightfully theirs."

"She's a thief!" said Petal.

"She's a glutton!" said Marcia.

"She's brilliant," said Georgia, real admiration in her eyes.

"And how," agreed Rebecca.

But before we could continue our debate on whether Durinda's cat was a crook or a genius, Zinnia inched over to Dandruff, lay down on her stomach, and whispered in Dandruff's ear.

Dandruff ceased her licking and cocked an ear as Zinnia whispered whatever she whispered. We could almost see the gears spinning in Dandruff's great cat brain.

Then Dandruff shook her head.

So Zinnia whispered something else, more urgently.

Dandruff cocked the other ear, looked as though she were thinking, then shook her head again.

So Zinnia whispered a third time, the most urgent whispering of all.

This time, Dandruff seemed to listen very closely, then nodded sharply and exited the room.

"What did you say to her?" Jackie asked.

"First," Zinnia said, "I told her that if she kept eating like that, she'd grow to be so fat people would take her for a tiger. But that didn't bother her very much. In fact, she rather seemed to like the idea."

"So what did you say next?" Marcia wanted to know.

"I told her that her sisters would starve if she kept eating all their food," Zinnia said, "but that didn't seem to have any effect on her either."

"So what did you say the last time?" Annie pressed.

"I said," Zinnia said, "that only wretched dogs ate everything in sight like she was doing, and she'd better stop it before we all started calling her Dog instead of Dandruff. That did the trick."

We could well imagine that if you were a cat, being called Dog would be the worst thing that could possibly happen to you. Unless of course you were to get eaten by one; a dog, that is.

"And that really did it?" Durinda asked.

"Oh, yes," Zinnia said solemnly. "Dandruff assures me she'll only freeze the other cats now if they're about to do something dangerous and she needs to save their lives."

Of course, none of us believed all that stuff about the conversation between Zinnia and Dandruff. Oh, we did believe that Zinnia had said what she'd said she'd said. But we certainly didn't believe that any of the cats understood the things Zinnia said or that the cats actually talked back to her. A kid being able to communicate with cats? Get real.

But it was nice that once the other cats became unfrozen, Dandruff didn't try to freeze them again.

* * * * * * * *

After serving us a dinner of PBJs, Durinda was upset.

Not about the PBJs. Durinda had already given up feeling any guilt that she couldn't feed us proper hot meals because Carl was depressed over love. No, Durinda was upset about her power.

"Do you think it's possible," she wondered, "to reject a power? I'm not sure I want to keep mine."

"Why ever not?" Rebecca wanted to know. "It seems to me like it'd be a great power to have. If you want the last slice of pizza? Just freeze everyone else and then go for it. Why, when I get my power, I hope it's as nifty as the one you wound up with."

"You would think that, wouldn't you?" Durinda said. Then she turned to the rest of us. "But it's scary. Look what just happened with Dandruff and the other cats. They could have starved! It's too much power for one person, or cat, to have. What if I use it for evil?"

"Get a paper and pencil," Annie ordered Marcia with a snap of her fingers.

"What's the paper and pencil for?" Jackie wanted to know.

"It's for making a pro-and-con list," Annie said.

"What's a pro-and-con list?" Zinnia asked as Marcia returned.

"On one side of the sheet," Annie said, "we'll list the pros: all the good things about Durinda's power. On the other side, we'll list the cons: all the bad stuff."

Georgia insisted we start with the con side first.

CONS

- Too much power for one of us to have (Rebecca)
- It will go to her head (Georgia)
- It will go to her head, she will freeze us all so she can save all the best food for herself, and they will find our skinny bodies in the gutter! (Petal)

PROS

- If some selfish person is buying up all the good cat food at the supermarket, you can freeze them before they take the last bag (Marcia)
- It would be great fun to try it on the McG, even if there's no good reason to freeze her (Jackie)
- It's too good a power to pass up (Zinnia)

"I think it's pretty obvious," Annie concluded, "as Zinnia points out, it's too good a power for you to give up. And I'm sure there must be other great uses for it. We just haven't thought of them yet."

You may think it astonishing that we didn't list the one thing that Durinda's power would be perfect for. Or, if you're not thinking that now, you *will* think it when we finally do realize the perfect use for Durinda's power. What can we say in our defense? *There were 9 more shopping days, 8 more shopping days, 7 more . . .*

And we had talking refrigerators that would no longer do their jobs properly and the subject of Love, with a capital *L*, too much on the mind.

CHAPTER FIVE

All of the horrible things that had happened to us—and having our parents disappear, or die, certainly numbered among them—felt like nothing compared to what we did to another human being on Valentine's Day.

It was at last February 14, and we had all entered the third-grade classroom at the Whistle Stop with great excitement in our bellies. Today was the day we were going to give Will all the lovely cards we'd prepared! Today we would finally learn which of us he loved best!

Naturally the McG, being the McG, waited until the last hour of the school day to hold our celebration.

"We always do things alphabetically," the McG said, "meaning that the Eights always get to go first. But why should things remain so? Today, we'll go in reverse alphabetical order. Mandy Stenko will give her cards out, followed by Will Simms, and then I have a little something for everyone. Only after we have gone will the Eights go."

So that's what happened.

Mandy looked so proud of herself as she moved from desk to desk depositing what were obviously handmade valentines, each one taken from a beautiful, shiny red bag. She even had one for the McG.

We looked at ours. Each valentine had one of our names on it—she even gave the right valentine to each Eight—and all the names were in glittery script. She must have drawn our names in glue first and then poured glitter over the glue and shook off the excess. Under each of our names, she'd written the same exact thing on all of our cards: *Thank you for being my friend.*

It was then we knew that we had done something wrong. Very wrong. But perhaps we weren't the only ones?

Then it was Will's turn.

The ones he gave us were very nice. They were decorated with stickers that looked like hockey pucks, the many pucks placed close together to form big hearts. And he'd used stickers that looked like hockey sticks to spell out the letters in our names. He too got our names right. Well, of course he did. He was Will Simms, after all. And he too had a card for the only other non-Eight student in our class, plus one for the teacher.

Oh, this was bad. Very bad.

Then it was the McG's turn.

She gave cards to Will and Mandy first. Will's had a picture of a hockey rink on it. Apparently, the McG had finally gotten the memo that Will hated soccer. As for the card she gave Mandy, after Mandy opened it, she blushed and put it in her desk. It wasn't until later that it occurred to us that she was trying to spare our feelings. But before she could finish putting it away, we saw what the McG had written: *To Mandy Stenko, my very best student.*

Then the McG gave out much smaller cards to each of us. Instead of our names, she had merely written *Eight* on each in boring black marker, and the cards were nothing special, but still . . .

Oh, this was very bad. This was so bad, it could not have been worse.

"Well, Zinnia?" the McG prompted. "Why haven't you started handing out your cards yet? I'm surprised. You Eights are always so quick to be first at anything."

Zinnia could avoid it no longer. *We* could avoid it no longer.

She rose from her seat and, lickety-split, raced to Will's desk and deposited the valentine she'd so lovingly made, then raced back to her own chair.

Then Rebecca did the same.

Then Petal.

Then Marcia.

Then Jackie.

Then Georgia.

Then Durinda.

For once, Annie was the last to go.

We had put so much time into these—all that red and pink paper, all that glitter, all those feathers and sequins—but now all we felt was awful and ashamed.

"Aren't you forgetting someone, Eights?" the McG asked expectantly. "Or some*ones?*"

Eight heads shook from side to side. Eight heads hung in shame.

"What is *wrong* with you children?" the McG practically shrieked. "Never mind that you left out one of your own classmates—how could you leave out *me?*"

We stole a glance over at Mandy. She was sitting in her seat, quietly crying. It was as though the lovely

valentines she'd received from Will and the McG didn't matter.

She looked up at us, tears staining her cheeks. "Why do you all hate me so?" she asked simply.

We could have lived with the McG's shrieking—she'd never once been kind to us—but we couldn't live with the look of sadness on Mandy's face, nor could we live with the way we saw Will looking at us now. We'd hurt another child. It was too much.

Before the rest of us knew what was happening, before Will and Mandy and the McG could realize what was happening to them, Durinda rapidly tapped three times against her leg and sharply pointed her finger, doing the whole thing three times in one great blur of motion until she'd frozen our classmates and teacher.

"So what do we do now?" Marcia asked.

"I don't know," Durinda said. "I just couldn't bear it any longer, having them look at us like that."

It felt odd, having just us Eights talking in a classroom where our teacher and classmates normally talked too. It was like being home alone, except not.

"I don't know that we *can* do anything," Annie said. "Sure, Durinda froze them, but they won't stay frozen forever. And we can't erase their memories. They'll all remember what we've done."

"Even I feel bad," Rebecca said.

And so we waited, the clock on the wall loudly ticking away all the while, for our teacher and classmates to come back to us.

Luckily, they came back at exactly the same time.

Unluckily, the McG continued right where she'd left off.

"Don't you *know*," she said, "that it's awful to leave out any child on Valentine's Day? When I was a child, I was often left out. And let me tell you, *that hurt!*"

We might have guessed that the McG's obsession with Valentine's Day stemmed from some sadness in her childhood.

"We're sorry," we said to the McG.

Then we turned to Mandy, speaking the exact same words at the exact same time because we were each feeling the exact same thing: "We're sorry. We didn't mean to hurt you. We'll make it up to you somehow."

But knowing that the McG was upset over her own childhood didn't help us now, for the McG was shrieking at us again. "This is the last straw! I'm marching you down to Principal Freud's office and we're calling your parents! Mandy, take over the classroom!"

* * * * * * * *

Principal Freud was very bald. He was so bald, we'd often thought that if a single hair tried to grow on his head, it would die of loneliness.

But Principal Freud's hair, or lack of it, didn't matter right now since Principal Freud was disappointed in us.

It's not great when an adult is angry at you, like the McG was with us. But it's far worse when an adult is disappointed in you, particularly when it's an adult you respect.

"I'm afraid," Principal Freud informed us, "that I'm going to have to side with Mrs. McGillicuddy on this one. Your parents will have to come in."

This was badder than bad.

It would be one thing if Principal Freud sent a note home; Annie could always forge a reply. It would be one thing if he insisted one of our parents call him; Annie could fake Daddy's voice. But none of us could pretend to be Daddy in person. We were all too short. Besides, they'd seen him before.

"Mommy is at home with a terrible tummy virus," Annie said. "You wouldn't want to catch it. It's nasty. And our father is modeling in France."

These were our standard lies to tell whenever we were called upon to produce our parents.

"I'm sorry," Principal Freud said, "but that simply will not do. I insist on speaking with some family member—"

Annie opened her mouth.

"—who also happens to be an adult," Principal Freud finished, shutting Annie's mouth.

Hmm . . . a family member who was also an adult?

Aunt Martha? Uncle George?

Nah and nah.

They'd never liked kids. Besides, we were pretty sure they lived too far away.

"Can I use your phone?" Annie asked Principal Freud as the McG glared. "I need to call our uncle."

Seven heads swiveled toward Annie. What was she talking about?

"Of course," Principal Freud said, moving the phone toward her.

"Can we have some privacy?" Annie asked, looking meaningfully at Principal Freud and the McG. "Our uncle is, well, a bit odd. He gets very nervous talking on the phone if there are people he doesn't know listening in."

Principal Freud gave Annie a strange look, but then

he indicated the McG should follow as he exited his own office, shutting the door behind them.

"Pete," we heard Annie whisper into the phone after she punched in the number for Pete's Repairs and Auto Wrecking, "we have a huge favor to ask of you . . ."

Annie had called on our savior. Annie had called Pete the mechanic.

* * * * * * * *

Pete was our father's mechanic. Previously, we'd tricked him into teaching Annie how to drive Mommy's Hummer. Then we'd called him to help us when someone tampered with that same Hummer after Will's birthday party. Now we'd called on him to pretend he was our uncle.

"Pete Huit here," Pete said, shaking first the McG's hand and then Principal Freud's.

We looked at Pete oddly. He was using a fake British accent, just like Annie did whenever she impersonated Daddy.

Never mind the bad accent, though, for Pete had done us proud. Over his usual outfit of ill-fitting jeans and navy blue T-shirt against which his belly bulged, he'd put on a wide and wild tie that looked like it was knotted mostly correctly and he'd even donned a man's jacket, although the sleeves were a bit short. It looked like it might have come from a tux.

"Now what have my girls got up to this time?" Pete asked, taking a seat.

"*Your* girls?" the McG asked pointedly.

"My brother's girls, my girls," Pete said. "We're just one big happy family."

Pete was probably sorry he'd asked, because the McG proceeded to tell him the whole story, nearly coming to angry tears again when she got to the part about receiving no valentines when she was a child.

Now it was Pete's turn to look at us with disappointment.

"You hurt a classmate, did you?" he asked.

We nodded.

"Well," he said, his expression softening, "you girls have had an awful lot thrust on your plate lately."

Then Pete turned back to Principal Freud and the McG.

"My girls are sorry," he said, "but this has been just one huge mix-up. Of course the girls planned to bring valentines in for this Mandy Stenko. For their lovely teacher too," Pete added, lying through his teeth. "But— what, ho!—things have been insanely busy at their house lately. So, you see, they *made* the valentines; they just didn't *bring* the valentines."

"Are you quite certain of this, Mr., er, Pete Huit?" Principal Freud asked.

"Of course," Pete said. "What kind of children do you think we raise in the Huit family? They would never hurt another child intentionally, and I can assure you they never will again."

We all nodded at Pete, giving him our silent vow.

"But what about me?" The McG either sniffed or sniffled. It was hard to tell.

That's when Pete rose from his chair, lifted the McG's hand, and kissed the back of it. "Oh," he said with a wink, "who could forget you, ducks?" Pete looked back at Principal Freud. "Are we through here, then?" he asked.

"What? Oh, yes," Principal Freud said. "Except for . . ."

"What?" Pete waited patiently.

"It's just that . . . *jacket* you're wearing." Principal Freud blushed. "I've never seen anything like—"

"What? This old thing?" Pete proudly patted the left sleeve with his right hand. "It's an Armani."

Pete was out the door and we'd already started to trail after him—we still needed to thank him in private—when Principal Freud's voice stopped us.

"This Pete Huit," he whispered. "He doesn't sound like your dad, he doesn't look like him, and that jacket . . . Let's just say, he doesn't seem at all like your model dad."

"That's because he's not," Durinda said with a proud smile. "He's just Pete—I mean, Uncle Pete—and he's like no one else in our world."

CHAPTER SIX

We caught up to Pete in the parking lot.

"Thank you, Mr. Pete!" we shouted at him, one after another.

"My pleasure," he said, turning around to face us. "For some reason, even though I'm never even sure I should be doing it, I don't mind helping you lot."

We did notice that he'd stopped speaking with his fake British accent, which was a good thing. He was awful at it.

Still, we stared at him, sighing, happy in the moment.

Then we looked around and realized there was a new thing that was terribly wrong.

"Oh, no!" Petal cried, her lower lip starting to quiver. "The school day is over!"

"And that's a bad thing?" Pete's smile was easy. "I should think that after the day you lot have had, you'd be grateful to see it done."

"Of course," Annie said. "But what Petal means is that our school bus has departed, and it's done so without us."

"Maybe," Jackie suggested, "we could go back in the school and ask Principal Freud if he'll let us use his phone again so we can call a cab."

"You mean *cabs,*" Rebecca said testily. "And how many do you think we'll need to call?"

"Never mind that none of us has any money on her here," Georgia pointed out. "The checkbook is at home. The credit cards too."

"Wait a minute," Pete said. "You mean you don't have any way to get home?"

Eight heads shook no, Petal's head shaking the hardest as a tear tipped over her lower eyelid and traced its lonely way down her cheek.

"I suppose we could walk," Georgia suggested. "We walked up the driveway once. I suppose we could walk a few miles home." Georgia had been trapped in an avalanche one time and could be said to be the most adventurously outdoorsy among us.

"You can't *walk!*" Pete said. "Your house is ten miles from here!"

"It *is?*" eight voices said. We were shocked.

"I suppose there's nothing for it," he said. "I'll have to give you a lift." Then he smiled, as though a wonderful idea had just occurred to him. "Say, it is

Valentine's Day today, meaning tonight it's something like Valentine's Night, as it were. I don't suppose you're planning any sort of celebratory holiday dinner with, er, your parents?"

Eight heads shook no.

"Right," Pete said, as though he'd suspected as much. "Your father is still in the bathroom and your mother is off in France. Or was it the opposite?" He shook his head. "Anyway, I thought you might like to come home to have dinner at my house. My wife would love to have eight children over for dinner."

We somehow doubted that. No one except for our parents liked to feed us all at once—okay, Will's mother didn't mind either—and we suspected Mrs. Pete wouldn't like to have her own romantic Valentine's dinner interfered with.

Annie looked as though she were about to say no on our behalf when Petal grabbed on to one of her arms and Zinnia yanked on the other.

"Please!" Petal cried. "Pleasepleasepleasepleaseplease! I haven't had a hot meal in nearly two weeks!"

"You know the refrigerator is broken!" Zinnia said. "We'll all starve soon!"

Durinda looked offended, as though we were not giving her enough credit for the job she'd done feeding us under trying circumstances.

Pete, however, looked horrified.

"You mean you're not even getting proper meals anymore?" He didn't wait for an answer. "That settles it. You're *definitely* coming home with me. And afterward, I'll even take you home and fix your fridge for you."

We didn't believe he could fix what was wrong with Carl the talking refrigerator, but we were all grateful for the prospect of a home-cooked meal. Well, most of us were.

"Look at him," Rebecca muttered under her breath as Pete led us across the parking lot.

"I know," Georgia muttered right back at her. "Mrs. Pete probably only ever feeds him leg of lamb. We'll probably get stuck eating leg of lamb for our Valentine's dinner."

"Oh, do be quiet," Jackie said. "At least we'll be eating something other than PBJs."

"I resent—" Durinda began, but she never got to finish her objection because we had arrived in front of Pete's vehicle.

"It's a pickup truck," Marcia observed.

"Where's your great big van?" Annie asked.

Pete hit himself on the forehead with the palm of his hand. We suspected that that hurt.

"Oh, no!" he said. "I brought the pickup. I never

expected to be ferrying all eight of you around town. Not," he added, "that it's not a great honor."

We're pretty certain Annie was about to try again to reject Pete's kind offer, but Petal and Zinnia moved toward her so quickly, we suspect she didn't want to have her arms grabbed and yanked on again. So instead, she simply said, "Fine."

So that's how we found ourselves zipping through town on our way to have dinner at Pete's house with him and Mrs. Pete. We were all eight in the back of the pickup, because there wasn't enough room in the front cab with Pete for all eight, and it wouldn't have been fair for one or two of us to stay warm while the rest froze. So we sat together on the bed of the pickup, our hair whipping around us in the cold February wind.

"Are you sure this is legal?" Petal wondered as we all bounced along. "None of us is even wearing a seat belt."

"Who cares?" Durinda shouted with glee. "For once I don't have to worry about preparing dinner. Besides, I'm having fun!"

* * * * * * * *

Pete's house turned out to be a very small house, but there was something quite cozy about it.

"I've told the missus all about you lot," he said, holding the front door open for us.

We wondered just exactly what he'd told her.

Mrs. Pete was waiting inside, and she was everything you'd expect Pete's wife to look like: she had gray hair that was more salt than pepper, a well-fed belly that bulged against her navy blue T-shirt, and low-slung jeans hanging off her hips. The biggest difference between them was she was a lot shorter than he.

"You must be Annie," she said with a warm smile, taking Annie's hand.

Then she did the same with each of us in turn, placing the right name with the right girl.

"Pete's described you each so many times," she said. "It was like I knew you before I ever saw you."

We liked Mrs. Pete right away.

She led us inside, where a big fire blazed in the small fireplace.

"Dinner's just about ready," she announced.

That's when we noticed how good their house smelled. It smelled of home-cooked food. More than that, it smelled of love.

"We don't want to put you out," Annie said.

"We're used to PBJs," Rebecca added.

"It's no trouble," Mrs. Pete said. "I've always wanted a whole houseful of children."

"Haven't you any of your own?" Petal piped up.

"Sadly, no," Mrs. Pete said, looking very unhappy when she said it.

"I'll bet these people would give great presents to their kids," Zinnia whispered as the Petes, Mr. and Mrs., led us to their dining room table.

And so we ate Valentine's Day dinner with the Petes.

There was roast beef, which Pete carved himself. There were real mashed potatoes with enough gravy for everyone. They didn't even make us eat the salad, and for dessert there was fresh strawberry cream pie with enough whipped cream on it to satisfy even Rebecca. It was the best meal we'd had since before New Year's Eve. (Not to knock Durinda's cooking skills.)

When the last dish had been wiped clean and all

the dishes cleared away—we did help clear the table—
Mrs. Pete brought out a large book to show us. She
said it was a special book.

"As I said before," she said, "Pete has told me all
about you and he's told me about your, er, situation, or
at least what he thinks that situation might be. I think
this book might help."

"It looks like just an ordinary book," Marcia
observed. "Except it's very large."

"What is it?" Jackie wanted to know.

"Are there stories in it?" Zinnia asked.

"I hope they're scary stories," Georgia said.

"With lots of blood and guts," Rebecca added.

"I'm afraid not," Mrs. Pete said with an easy laugh.
"There are no scary stories here, but it is a very special book. It's called *The Mommy Catalog*."

"*The Mommy Catalog?*" Durinda asked. "I never
heard of such a thing."

"Oh, yes," Mrs. Pete said, opening the book and flipping the pages. "You can pick out any kind of mommy
you want from this book."

"Hey!" Jackie said. "That one is called the Tall
Mommy! I'll bet she'd come in very handy. You'd never
need a stepladder with her around!"

"What about the Soft Mommy?" Petal said. "She
looks like she'd be great for giving out hugs."

"The Silly Mommy looks like she'd only be fun for about a day," Rebecca said.

"Then we'd have to kick her out," Georgia added.

"The Funny Mommy doesn't look like she'd be half as funny as she probably thinks she is," Marcia observed.

"The Money Mommy could be cool," Annie said. "It'd be nice to not have to worry about handling the money anymore."

"The Money Mommy sounds good to me too," Zinnia said.

We all agreed that the Pretty Mommy, while pretty, wasn't the kind of mommy a person needed to have.

"Hey!" Durinda said suddenly, flipping the page. "That's *you,* Mrs. Pete! Isn't it?"

Mrs. Pete blushed.

We studied her picture in *The Mommy Catalog.* Underneath it, the legend read, *The Nice Mommy.*

We could see where that must be true.

"Is there a catalog like this for daddies too?" Jackie wanted to know.

"Oh, yes," Mrs. Pete said.

"And is . . . ?" Jackie jerked her head toward the fireplace, in front of which sat Pete in a wing chair, stroking the black cat that purred in his lap.

"Oh, yes," Mrs. Pete said. "He is. He's the Nice

Daddy." She cleared her throat, as though she were nervous about something. "Pete was wondering . . . that is, we've both been wondering . . . since your parents don't seem to be around anymore . . . would you like to come live with us for a bit?"

"You could even bring all your eight cats," Pete said from where he sat with his cat. "Old Felix here wouldn't mind the company."

"Nor would we," Mrs. Pete added. "This house may not look very large to you, but it has this funny habit of expanding to hold however many people are in it."

It was true.

When we'd first seen their house, we thought it looked small. In fact, if asked, we would have guessed we'd feel cramped inside. But that wasn't the case. It fit around us just fine.

"Think about it," Mrs. Pete suggested, then she left the room, probably to give us time to talk.

"Is Mommy in *The Mommy Catalog*?" Petal whispered.

"No," Annie said, flipping through all the pages. Then she did the same with *The Daddy Catalog*. "Daddy neither."

"I wonder what their pages would say if they were?" Marcia said.

"Mommy's would say *The Perfect Mommy*," Jackie said. "And Daddy's would say *The Perfect Daddy*."

"And then it would say *too bad they disappeared*," Georgia said.

"And after that, *or died*," Rebecca added.

Zinnia sighed big enough for all of us.

As Mrs. Pete returned to the table, we thought about what the Petes had offered us. Oh, did we think about it!

It would be so wonderful to be in a house with adults in it again.

It would be wonderful to have meals that smelled and tasted like the meal we'd had that night.

It would be wonderful to be surrounded by so much love.

But . . .

"No," Annie said, speaking for all of us, who agreed with her in spirit even while we felt bitter at the loss of the dream of the Petes.

"We would love to, truly we would," Annie went on. "But we simply can't. You see, if we stay here, we'll get too comfortable, and then . . ." Her voice trailed off.

"And then," Pete finished for her, "you might never figure out how to get your dad back from the bathroom and your mom back from France."

"Exactly," Annie said, clearly relieved that someone else had completed the sentence for her so she didn't have to lie directly to Mrs. Pete. Or tell the truth.

"I guess there's nothing else for it then," Pete said, gently removing Old Felix from his lap and rising. "It's time for me to run you lot home. I expect you've got some homework to do, not to mention two valentines to create, and morning will be here before you know it."

"Just remember," Mrs. Pete said, seeing us off at the door and giving each of us a kiss on the cheek, "our door is always open to you, and our offer will always stand."

CHAPTER SEVEN

We arrived home to a dark house and eight hungry cats.

"I'll put the kibble out," Jackie offered, "while Durinda shows Mr. Pete the fridge."

Pete had brought his toolbox with him, and we watched in the kitchen as he gently pulled Carl the talking refrigerator away from the wall so he could see what was going on with Carl's backside.

Pete was just taking his screwdriver out when we heard a loud thumping noise. We looked up to see a carrier pigeon beating its little body against the big picture window that looked out over the hill.

Durinda let the pigeon in and unfurled the tiny scroll from the silver tube that was attached to the carrier pigeon's leg. We all looked over her shoulder to read the message: *Everything still okay in there?*

Durinda wrote back for all of us: *As well as can*

be expected! Then she attached the message and released the carrier pigeon back out the window.

"Does that happen all the time?" Pete asked. "Carrier pigeons flying at your window bearing notes?"

"Often enough." Annie shrugged. "They're Daddy's friends. They used to visit all the time before he, er, went to the bathroom."

"We're pretty sure they're friendly pigeons," Petal told Pete. "We'd be scared of them otherwise."

Pete shook his head. "This is a strange house you're living in here." Then he went back to work on Carl.

After a while, he poked his head out. "This is the oddest thing," Pete said. "Your refrigerator is leaking water like crazy, and yet when I look inside it, I can't find anything wrong."

"Oh, there's something wrong with it all right," Rebecca said darkly.

"Or instead of *it*," Georgia corrected, "perhaps we should say there's something wrong with *him*."

"Him?" Pete looked at us questioningly.

We hadn't planned on telling Pete the truth about Carl. But it seemed wrong somehow, now that he was here, to let him go on wasting his time trying to fix Carl when Carl couldn't be fixed. Or at least not in any way Pete's toolbox could manage.

"Pete," Durinda said, "meet Carl, our talking refrig-erator."

"Refrigerator's can't—" Pete started to say.

"Don't insult me," Carl the talking refrigerator said to Pete, "I feel bad enough already."

"Oh." Pete looked at Carl. "I see."

"The thing is," Marcia said, "Carl the talking refrig-erator is in love with Betty."

"Who's Betty?" Pete wanted to know. "The talking dishwasher?"

"Of course not," Rebecca said testily.

"She's our robot," Georgia added.

"Of course she is," Pete said.

"But Betty doesn't seem to love Carl in return," Zinnia said.

"And Carl is very heartbroken over that fact," Petal said.

"You can't be 'very' heartbroken," Rebecca said. "Heartbroken is one of those things you either are or you aren't. There's no 'very' about it."

"Maybe," Pete said, "Carl needs to pretend he doesn't like Betty any longer, and then she'll come after him."

"How do you mean?" Annie asked.

"Well," Pete said, "do you ever hold on to one of your cats too hard, and then, before you know it, that cat is doing everything she can to get away?"

Eight heads nodded. We'd all done that: held on too hard.

"But then," Pete went on, "did you ever notice how if you don't go after the cat but instead sit quietly in one spot, eventually the cat will jump right into your lap and stay there?"

Huh. We'd never thought to try that.

"Call Betty in here," Pete suggested. Then he turned to Carl. "And you, when she comes in, you pretend you don't even notice her." Then Pete looked up at the ceiling. "I can't believe," he said, "that I'm talking to a refrigerator."

"At least," Jackie pointed out, "this refrigerator can talk back."

"Yes," Durinda agreed. "It would be awful if you were just some crazy person talking to appliances that couldn't hold down their ends of the conversation."

So Marcia and Zinnia went off to get Betty. They were gone a long time and we guessed it was because when you told Betty to go to the kitchen, she often went to the bathroom instead.

At last, Betty entered the room. She looked as though she were about to head right back out again—nope, nothing to see here—when she paused as though listening for something.

Carl remained silent. If it were possible for refrigerators to ignore things, it sure looked as though Carl were ignoring Betty.

Betty inched closer to Carl.

Carl continued to ignore. In fact, he began whistling a tune. And it wasn't a love tune, like you'd expect. Oh, no. It was the kind of tune you'd whistle if you were mountain climbing and had all the time in the world to get to the top.

Betty inched so close to Carl, she was right in front of him. Then she took her mechanical head and rubbed it against his door handle. It was kind of like when our cats rubbed against our legs.

Carl stopped whistling.

Carl started to hum.

Gently moving Betty to one side, Pete opened the refrigerator and the freezer both at once. We looked inside: everything was freezing up nicely.

"Betty loves Carl!" we cried. "We can eat real food again!"

We looked at Pete, something like awe on our faces.

Who knew that Pete, in addition to being a crack-erjack mechanic, was such an expert on love?

"Now that that's settled," Pete said, "what do you say you get down to making those valentines for the classmate whose feelings you hurt and that awful McG person?"

So that's what we did.

Once again, we got out the pink and red construc-tion paper, the scissors and paste, the glitter and the feathers and the sequins.

With Pete supervising, we were a lot less likely to get in paste fights; Rebecca didn't even try running with the scissors; and our group crafts project was soon completed.

Just as we were putting our new valentines next to the front door so we wouldn't forget to bring them to school the next morning, Zinnia, who we hadn't even noticed leave, reentered the room.

"Dandruff is doing it again," she informed us.

Oh no.

Jackie jerked her head in Pete's direction, as though trying to tell Zinnia, *Not in front of Pete!*

But it was too late.

"Who's Dandruff?" Pete wanted to know. "And what's she doing again?"

We looked at one another. We really hadn't planned on telling him. But then, he knew now we had a talking refrigerator, and that the talking refrigerator was in love with our robot. So how much worse could it be?

"Dandruff is Durinda's cat," Georgia said.

"Durinda can freeze people by tapping her hand against her leg three times and pointing her finger at them as though her finger were a gun," Rebecca said.

"Except it doesn't work on me," Zinnia said.

"And now I'm thinking," Marcia observed, "if it doesn't work on Zinnia, there might be other people it doesn't work on. We just don't know who those people are yet."

"And Dandruff," Jackie said, giving in to the idea of telling Pete all about it since all the others were, "being Durinda's cat, shares Durinda's power."

Pete looked at us. "You're joking, right?"

"Oh, no." Annie shook her head. "I can assure you we are not."

So we led Pete to the cat room, where we were just in time for Pete to witness Dandruff raise her tiny right paw, tap it against her hind leg rapidly three times, and sharply point it at Anthrax, freezing her where she stood.

"Dandruff says she's just getting even with Anthrax for always being so bossy," Zinnia said quietly, but none of us were paying attention to her. Thankfully, Pete wasn't either. If he had been, he'd be right in thinking us a nutty family, what with having one of us saying she could talk with cats and all.

"If I hadn't seen it with my own eyes," Pete said, staring, "I'd have never believed it." Then he turned to Durinda. "And you can do this too?"

Shyly, Durinda nodded.

"This really is the craziest house," Pete said, looking around.

It was hard to argue with that.

Pete turned to Durinda again. "Ever try freezing yourself?" Pete wanted to know.

"God, no," Durinda said. "I'd be scared to. What if I never came back? Oh, dear," she said, as though a horrible thought had just struck her. "What if one night in my sleep, I get angry at something and accidentally tap my leg three times and then point at myself?"

"I don't think there's much chance of *that* happening," Rebecca scoffed.

"But Durinda's attitude *is* a problem," Georgia said.

"How do you mean?" Pete asked.

"I'm scared," Durinda admitted, "of using my

power. What if I do something wrong with it? We did time trials and discovered the longest I can freeze any of the others is just under an hour. But what if I mess up and freeze someone I don't mean to freeze and that person stays frozen forever?"

"See what we mean about her being scared all the time?" Georgia said.

"So we made her a pro-and-con list," Marcia said.

"Why don't you get it?" Annie suggested. "Let's see what Mr. Pete thinks."

"Would you like Durinda to freeze you," Rebecca offered to Pete, "so you can see what it's like?"

Pete held up his hands. "No, thank you."

Marcia returned with the list.

When we showed it to him, Pete said, "You left one item off your list."

"We did?" Annie was offended. She'd been very proud of that list.

"Oh, yes," Pete said. "Say you have someone truly awful in your world. And say you either have to get away from that person or freeze them just long enough so you can get around them. I'll bet, in a situation such as that, Durinda's power would come in mighty handy."

And then at last it struck us: what we could do

with Durinda's power, who we should get her to freeze. It amazed us that we hadn't seen it sooner, but now:

Oh.

Oh, my.

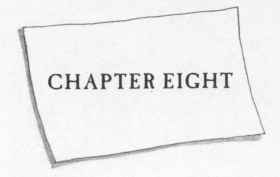

CHAPTER EIGHT

Back in January, our evil neighbor the Wicket had paid us a visit, bearing a fruitcake. Annie had told her that Mommy was working on something top secret. While we were out at Will's birthday party, the Wicket had tampered with our Hummer, ensuring we wouldn't arrive home until after she'd had the chance to toss Mommy's private study in search of the Top Secret file. When Pete fixed our Hummer and we arrived home early, she was still there, but we never saw her, nor did we catch her red-handed. Instead, all we found was the Top Secret folder.

It had been empty.

Ever since then, we'd waited for the Wicket to leave her own house so we could search it. So we could find out what she'd stolen from the Top Secret folder. So maybe we could discover a clue to the disappearance of our parents.

But she never went out anywhere.

Now Pete had given us the means, the idea of how we could get around the Wicket: we could freeze her.

But that night, after Pete left, we were too tired to set out on our dangerous mission. We'd had a long day and night already, and it seemed to us that such a thing would require keeping all of our wits about us.

Even Rebecca's.

So instead, we got a good night's sleep.

Then the next morning, we couldn't do anything right away, because first we had to go to school to deliver the valentines we'd made under Pete's supervision.

When we arrived at school, the McG was obviously still angry with us. She didn't even say hello as we took our seats, which felt odd. At the very least, we could usually get a *hello* out of her.

"Please turn to page seventy-five in your—" the McG started to say, but Annie cut her off.

"We have something for you," Annie said.

Then we trooped up to the McG's desk and deposited the eight valentines we had made for her.

The hearts we had made for her were small, we must admit, and each one said the same thing. In boring black marker, each of us had written, *Happy Valentine's Day to Mrs. McGillicuddy: You are a teacher.*

"Well," she said and sniffed after reading them all, "that is at least something."

"We have one for Mandy too," Annie said.

"*Just* one?" the McG said.

"Yes," Annie said.

When we looked over at Mandy, she looked as though she might start to cry again, so Zinnia hastily added, "It's just one, but it is a doozy."

Then we went out into the hallway where we'd left our valentine so no one in the classroom would see it before we were ready. It took all eight of us to carry it in. We'd had a devil of a time getting it to school on the bus.

We presented the giant heart to Mandy.

Mandy read aloud the words we'd written:

"'For Mandy Stenko: Thank you for being our friend.'"

She smiled so brightly, honestly, there are no words for how bright that smile was. Then she added, "Oh, look: you even each all signed your name to it, and you did it using glitter."

We had.

Now there were tears in Mandy's eyes again, only this time they looked to be tears of joy.

We didn't get it. We didn't understand why Mandy Stenko, who we'd always not liked very much and who we'd been sure didn't like us at all, should care if we thought of her as our friend or not.

And yet, apparently, she did.

It was a puzzle.

Still, we felt good in that moment, good that we'd made her feel better.

* * * * * * * *

When we arrived home from school, we quickly tossed our backpacks inside the door and headed over to the Wicket's house. We didn't even change out of our yellow plaid uniforms.

The Wicket's house looked normal enough from the outside, but it was much smaller than ours. And tidy. We thought *too tidy*.

Seven of us hid around the side of the house, our

heads peeking around the corner, one on top of the other, as Durinda stood on the stoop and rang the doorbell.

We saw the Wicket when she answered the door. She always looked the same: like a toadstool, short enough to be a child, with coal black eyes, a fright of spiky yellow hair, a very plump body, and short legs. And she always wore the same clothes: khaki pants and a red shirt with polka dots.

Before the Wicket could even say a word, Durinda tapped her leg rapidly three times and sharp-pointed at our evil neighbor.

We had all been secretly worried that the Wicket would turn out to be one of the people Durinda couldn't freeze. And then what would we do? But such was not the case.

The Wicket froze solid in her own doorway.

"Come on!" Durinda whispered to all of us with a gesture of her hand.

We hurried to the front stoop and followed Durinda, all of us careful not to touch the Wicket as we slithered around her frozen body and into her home.

The Wicket's and the Petes' homes may both have been small on the outside, but that's all they shared in common. Inside, they were far different. Where the Petes' house had smelled like love and all things wonderful, this place smelled like fruitcake, like all the person who lived in it ever did was make wretched fruitcakes.

And everything about the place was crooked.

The bare floors, without a comforting rug in sight, were slanted. The walls, painted an ugly mud color, came at you at odd angles. Even the pictures on the walls weren't hung straight.

"Come on," Annie said urgently. "We don't have time to stand around here all day just looking!"

"But isn't it fascinating?" Marcia observed.

"I've never been in an evil person's home before," Petal said.

"It is kind of nice," Rebecca added.

"I don't know about nice," Annie said, "although I'll agree it is fascinating in a purely scientific sort of way."

"But we'd better start searching," Durinda finished

for Annie, Annie having been distracted like the rest of us by sheer fascination. "We have no idea how long the Wicket will remain frozen in the doorway, and we have a job to do!"

"Where shall we look first?" Jackie asked.

"If the Wicket had a cat," Zinnia said, "I could ask it to tell me where the best place might be."

We ignored her.

"Mommy has her private study," Durinda said, "for doing important things."

"I suspect an evil person might have such a place too," Georgia suggested.

"Only she'd have it in some ugly place," Rebecca added with glee.

"Then we should check the basement," Petal said, fear in her eyes. Petal had a great fear of basements, for that was where all the spiders tended to gather.

But even Petal didn't want to be left upstairs alone with the frozen Wicket, so she followed us as we located the basement door and began our descent down the long and rickety wooden staircase.

We were lucky to have Annie leading us because she kept a cool head about her. It was Annie who noticed that the sixth and seventh steps were missing and cautioned us to be careful as we jumped down from the fifth to the eighth.

"She probably keeps them like that on purpose to trick intruders into breaking their nosy little legs," Rebecca said, as if she would know.

"The sixth and seventh steps," Marcia said. "Six and seven make thirteen, considered by some to be an unlucky number. Do you think it might be symbolic of something?"

"I don't think the Wicket thinks that deeply about things," Jackie said.

At last we were at the bottom of the stairs.

It felt as though it'd taken us forever to get there, but we'd had to be careful in case the Wicket had removed any more steps.

We only had the light from the open doorway at the top of the stairs to guide us, and it was rather dark down there. But then Annie found a cord hanging from the middle of the ceiling and pulled on it. Suddenly, a naked light bulb exposed the room, giving it an eerie yellow glow.

And there before us, looking not at all like Mommy's beautiful workspace, was the Wicket's desk.

It was gray metal, the color of a gun, and all around it was a barbed-wire fence.

It was a good thing we had never listened when Carl the talking refrigerator encouraged us to eat more, for now we were all skinny enough to snake our way through those nasty wires without getting scratched.

"How do you think the human toadstool gets through all of this?" Marcia wondered. "The Wicket's not skinny like we are."

"Her legs aren't long enough to go over it," Jackie said.

"And she can't fit under it," Zinnia added.

"Maybe she knows bad magic," Petal suggested, "and can just make it all disappear whenever she wants to?"

It was a puzzle.

We shrugged and then focused our attention on the more pressing matters at hand.

And there, right on the Wicket's desk, was her diary.

We knew this because the crooked handwritten letters on the front of the book said *My Diary*.

"Hurry!" Petal said. "I fear our time is running out . . . and I swear I can hear things crawling around down here!"

"Should we steal it?" Rebecca suggested.

"'Fraid not," Annie said. "As soon as the Wicket comes to and finds it missing, she'll know where to look."

"Too bad," Zinnia said. "It would have made a nice souvenir, almost like a present."

"Read it quickly then!" Petal urged Annie, ignoring Zinnia.

"If the entries are dated," Marcia suggested, "maybe you should go straight to the date when she broke into our home."

We had to admit: it was an excellent suggestion.

So that's what Annie did, flipping straight to the correct date in January.

Tonight I broke into the Eights' home and searched Lucy Huit's office. One of her stupid children—I can never remember which one is which—had let slip that she was working on something top secret. Everyone knows about Lucy Huit's experiments into unlocking the key to eternal life. I WANT TO live FOREVER! But, alas and alack, all my brilliant schemes were frustrated. The folder was empty. Perhaps one of our enemies got there first?

That was the end of that particular entry.

Annie read us a few more, but they were all the same: the Wicket raving about the empty folder, going on and on about the frustration of it all and "enemies." She really did sound like she might be nuts.

"The Wicket really wants to live forever," Annie said.

"What an awful thought," Jackie said with a shudder, "the idea of the Wicket living forever."

"We'd better get out of here," Durinda reminded us.

Then we placed the book back where we found it, lining up the edges with where they'd been; snaked out through the barbed wire; raced up the stairs—careful to stretch over the missing sixth and seventh steps—and slithered back around the still-frozen Wicket.

Then we ran all the way home.

CHAPTER NINE

What did it all mean?

We wondered.

"Why would the Top Secret folder have been empty before the Wicket even got to it?" Marcia wanted to know. "It doesn't make any sense."

"The Wicket's diary mentioned 'enemies,'" Petal said. "Maybe some other even eviler person snuck in here before she did and cleared out the folder first?"

"But that doesn't make sense either," Marcia said.

"Marcia's right," Jackie said. "The Wicket was watching the house so closely. She knew when we'd be out and she tampered with our car. Surely she would have noticed if someone else were nosing around our house too."

"Top Secret folder that should contain important papers but doesn't, new enemies who may or may not be lurking in the bushes." Zinnia grabbed the sides of her own head. "I feel like my head is going to explode!"

"All that means," Rebecca said, "is that you're not handling all this very well."

"But it doesn't tell us what anything else means," Georgia said.

"Maybe everything just means it's time for me to make dinner now?" Durinda said. "At least Carl is working properly again."

"I'll tell you what it all means," Annie said triumphantly. "It means our mother was—*is*—a bleeding genius!"

"'Bleeding'?" Marcia questioned. "Isn't that a British term? Are you sure we're not? British, I mean."

Annie ignored her.

"What I mean is," Annie said, "just think about it. If Mommy was working on something top secret involving people living forever, she was no doubt smart enough to know that other people, maybe even evil people, would do anything in their power to learn what that secret was. So what did she do? She left an *empty* Top Secret folder *on purpose,* to throw people off the track!"

We were in awe.

Mommy really *was* a genius.

"You're right," Durinda said, breaking our stunned silence. "Mommy's brain should be in the Smithsonian."

"But then," Marcia said, "if everything Annie says is right, then the Wicket isn't any real threat to us. She doesn't know anything, so how could she be? Besides which, if she had any idea where Mommy and Daddy had gone off to, she'd be chasing them because she'd still want to steal Mommy's secret to life. She doesn't know anything!"

"Yea!" Petal said. "We don't have to be afraid of the Wicket anymore!"

"Yea!" Zinnia added. "The Wicket doesn't know any more about anything than we do!"

"I don't care if the Wicket *doesn't* really have any information," Annie said. "You know how her type is: she'll keep messing with our lives and getting in the way. I say we get rid of her."

"You mean kill her?" Rebecca asked.

"She does give me the creeps," Petal said, exchanging her cheers for shudders. "All that barbed wire. People who booby-trap their homes are *not* to be trusted."

"No, not *kill* her," Annie said. "But I do think we should get her out of the way for as long as possible. And I know just how to do it."

* * * * * * * *

It had long since turned dark when we approached the Wicket's house again. In the intervening hours, we'd changed out of our school uniforms, eaten a hot meal, and made a run in the Hummer to the supermarket. At the supermarket, it took us a while to find the item we wanted, but now we were armed with exactly what we needed.

This time, instead of hiding while Durinda knocked, we all stood on the Wicket's stoop as a unit. Durinda was at the center, with Annie.

"Yes?" The Wicket answered the door. She eyed Durinda suspiciously. "Didn't you already visit me once recently?"

"Here." Durinda held out our offering before the Wicket could say anything more along those lines.

"What's that?" the Wicket said.

"Don't you recognize it?" Durinda held the heavy dish out farther. "It's a fruitcake. You kindly brought one to us the last time you visited, and we thought we should return the favor."

"Oh, yes," Rebecca said. "We definitely wanted to return it."

We hoped the Wicket didn't notice when Annie kicked Rebecca.

"It's the same fruitcake I gave you?" the Wicket asked.

"Of course not," Annie said, visibly miffed. "We don't believe in re-gifting."

"Of course we know it isn't as nice as yours was," Jackie said, "because we had to buy ours in a store."

"But we hoped you would think," Zinnia said, "that it's the gesture that counts."

At last, the Wicket took the fruitcake from Durinda.

Thank heavens, we thought. Another minute and Durinda would have dropped the heavy thing.

"Aren't you going to invite us in?" Durinda said. "We were hoping to enjoy some of that fruitcake with you."

"You know," Zinnia piped up, "we are neighbors."

"I suppose so," the Wicket said. "I'm not used to sharing my fruitcake." She guarded the dish jealously.

"Of course not," Annie said, as we all slithered past the Wicket and crossed the threshold. "We only want tiny slices. And if you don't want to, you don't even have to give us that."

"My," Georgia said as we all gazed around at the slanted floors without a comforting rug in sight, the ugly mud-colored walls that came at you at odd angles, and the crooked pictures on the walls as though we were seeing it for the first time, "what a lovely home you have here."

"We wish our home were more like this," Rebecca said.

"Fruitcake always makes me so thirsty," Jackie said. "Do you think you might bring us something to drink when you serve us ours?"

"You expect liquid refreshments too?" the Wicket demanded.

Eight heads nodded politely while inside we were thinking her very selfish not to offer us something to drink on her own when we'd gone and bought her such a fine fruitcake.

"What would you like to drink then?" the Wicket asked. "Coffee?"

"No, not *coffee*," Rebecca said. "We don't drink *coffee*."

"Of course we don't," Georgia said. "Haven't you noticed we're children?"

"Actually, I do drink coffee," Annie said, "you know, being the oldest. But I think water will be fine for all of us. We wouldn't want to put you out."

"No, we wouldn't want that," Jackie said.

"I'm not even sure if I have eight glasses," the Wicket grumbled under her breath as she headed off toward the kitchen, fruitcake gripped tightly in hand.

If there's one thing we have learned, it's that you shouldn't mutter or grumble under your breath when the people you are mumbling or grumbling about can hear you.

With the Wicket in the next room, we were able to spring into action.

Or, you could say, we were able to spring into talking.

Loudly.

"Gee," Annie said, yelling at the top of her lungs so probably people in the next town could hear her, never mind the Wicket, who was just in the next room. She was reciting her lines from the script she'd prepared and had us all memorize. "That was awful when some unknown person broke into our home a few weeks back."

"It really was," Durinda shouted.

"When we got home and found Mommy's private study had been entered, I thought I was going to have a heart attack," Georgia said.

"And to think," Jackie said, "whoever that awful person was, they took whatever was in Mommy's Top Secret folder."

"It's a good thing," Marcia said, "that whoever it was, they didn't know about the *other* folder."

The hairs stood up on the backs of our necks. It

was almost as though we could see the Wicket's ears perk up, hear her tiny little brain saying, *Wait a minute here. What* other *folder?*

She'd probably write about it in her diary tonight.

"Oh, don't know it," Petal said, muffing her lines. Then she self-corrected to "I mean to say, don't I know it."

"The *other* folder is an amazing thing," Rebecca said.

"It's true," Zinnia said, "and Mommy is a genius for inventing it."

Again, it was as though we could hear the Wicket's thoughts thundering through the walls: *What* other *folder?*

"Yes," Annie said, "only Mommy would think to create a second folder, marked *Nothing*, in which she put all of her *real* information about making it so people could live forever if they want to."

"And where does Mommy keep that other folder?" Durinda asked. "Sometimes I forget these things."

"She keeps it in the same file drawer as the Top Secret folder," Georgia said. "But it's hidden all the way in the back, behind the drawer itself."

"It's a good thing it's safe," Jackie said.

"But how long will it stay that way?" Marcia wondered.

"That's true," Petal said. "We have to go to that . . . *thing* at school Monday night." Petal had been supposed to say that *science fair,* but apparently she'd forgotten that part.

"And Mommy is going with us," Rebecca said.

"What time does that, er, *thing* start at school?" Petal asked, thereby making up for her previous fumbles by raising an important point that hadn't been covered in Annie's script.

"Six o'clock," Annie said.

"Isn't that a bit early for a school function?" Rebecca asked.

"Well, it is still winter," Annie said, "so it will already be dark by six, a fine time for a school function."

"Yes, Mommy is going with us," Rebecca said, repeating her earlier line to get us back to the original script.

"Daddy too," Zinnia said.

"So there will be no one at home," Annie added, finishing up the last lines in our script, "to make sure no one breaks in and searches the house for the Nothing folder."

We all sighed loudly as if there was nothing to be done about it. When you have a choice between going to a *thing* at school or guarding a Top Secret folder containing information that could change life on this planet as we know it, you always have to go to the *thing*.

"I just hope no one breaks in while we're gone." Durinda ad-libbed a last line.

The Wicket returned then, bearing a tray with eight jelly glasses. Inside of each, there was about an inch of rusty-looking water.

Gee, do you think she could spare it?

"My," Annie said, looking at her wrist even though she wasn't wearing a watch. "How time flies when you're having fun."

"We need to get going now," Durinda said. "Gotta keep up with that old homework, you know."

"And of course, we have a *thing* to prepare for," Jackie said.

"Bye!" said Petal.

"Bye!" said Zinnia. "Thanks for the water!"

We don't think the Wicket noticed that we hadn't drunk any of her rusty old water.

She was too busy smiling an evil smile.

* * * * * * * *

"So what do we do now?" Durinda asked Annie once we were outside again.

"Now," Annie said with a smile, "we go home and make a *Nothing* folder."

CHAPTER TEN

It was Monday and we were playing in the schoolyard.

Our recesses at the Whistle Stop lasted forty-five minutes. Even when it was cold outside, as it still was, unless there was a blizzard or monsoon going on, we were expected to play outside the whole time. The benefits of fresh air and all that.

Will was with us, but Mandy was off to one side, playing by herself and occasionally eyeing us darkly.

"We don't get it," Annie said to Will, speaking for all of us. "Mandy used to act like she hated us, but she wanted us to give her a valentine; we gave her a big valentine, and now it seems as though she's back to hating us again."

"It is a puzzle," Durinda said.

"She just doesn't know what to make of you," Will said. "She never has."

"How do you mean?" Marcia asked.

"Well, it's like this," Will said. "Mandy's an only child."

"She *is?*" Jackie said.

"Yes," Will said, "just like me. You know, it can get lonely being an only child."

Huh. That was something we'd never thought about.

"Even I get lonely sometimes," Will went on. "And for someone like Mandy, well, I think she looks at all of you and gets jealous for what you have: each other. And she wants to be a part of it, but she doesn't know how and she figures you don't really need her because you have that special thing: each other."

Huh. Who would have ever dreamed anyone would be jealous of us? And who would have ever dreamed Will knew so much about child psychology?

Will really was a marvelous boy. He was probably the most marvelous boy who had ever lived.

Which reminded us . . .

"Will," Annie asked coyly, "we've been meaning to ask you: which of our valentines did you like the best?"

"Was it mine?" Petal asked.

"Mine?" Zinnia echoed.

"I'm pretty sure it had to be mine," Rebecca said. "Mine had a rocket blaster instead of some measly old arrow smashing through the heart."

Eight girls leaned forward with bated breath. We were finally about to learn which of us Will liked the best.

Will's expression was puzzled.

"Best?" he said. "I liked them all the same. I like all of *you* the same."

Huh. Now there was something we hadn't expected.

"How could I like one of you more than the others?" Will went on. "It would be like asking me to name my favorite star in the night sky."

Eight girls sighed, sighs of love. Now this was something we could live with.

It was hard, though, never having anyone else with whom to share what was going on in our lives. True, we had one another, and that was a lot. And sure, Pete sort of knew what was going on. But it wasn't the same as having someone like us, someone, say, like Will, who we could confide in. It was time for us to take a chance. It was time for us to trust a person out-

side of our own inner circle, and who better than some-one wise like Will?

So we all perfectly understood why Annie said:

"Will, hold on to your hat." Even though he wasn't wearing a hat. "We have something to tell you . . ."

By the time recess was over, Will knew everything: about our parents' disappearance, or death; about the first note and the carrier pigeons; about the powers and the gifts; about the Wicket and the Top Secret folder. He even knew what we were planning for that night.

"I can't believe all this!" he said, stunned, when we'd finally stopped talking. "This has been going on since New Year's Eve. How did you ever keep all of this to yourselves? You Eights are amazing!"

Eight pairs of feet shuffled in modesty.

"Wow," Will said, "I'd sure love to be there when the Wicket breaks into your house again tonight . . ."

Which was how it happened that Will *was* there.

We'd had him call his mother and inform her our parents had okayed us inviting him over for a play date. He came home with us on the bus. After we introduced him to Carl the talking refrigerator and Betty, the love of Carl's life, we all sat down to the warm early dinner Durinda had prepared with Jackie's help.

It was odd eating dinner at four in the afternoon, but it was nice having nine of us at the table.

Will thought everything about us—Annie being able to handle the finances, Durinda being an ace in the kitchen—was so cool. He even thought it was cool when we had Dandruff demonstrate for him how she could freeze all of the cats except Zither.

"I can't believe you all live like this!" Will said. "And nobody knows it!"

Except for Will. And Pete, sort of.

It was great seeing our lives through Will's eyes. When Pete had been here the night he helped fix Carl and made us make the valentines, he hadn't stopped liking us over it, but we knew he thought the way we lived was odd. Probably because he said as much. But Will? He just loved it all.

Then it was time to stop playing and get down to serious business.

"Durinda," Annie said, "prepare the Hummer."

Will raised his eyebrows and pointed at Annie. "She drives?"

We guessed we hadn't told him that part.

"Oh, yes," Jackie said.

"But not as well as she thinks she does," Georgia muttered, earning a smack from Annie, who'd heard the mutter.

Once we were all in the Hummer and Annie was inching down the driveway, Will started looking a little green around the edges.

"Are you sure Annie knows what she's doing?" Will asked.

"Most of the time." Rebecca shrugged as Annie nearly ran over the mailperson, who was making a late delivery.

"Don't worry," Marcia said. "We're not going far."

"Just around the corner," Jackie said, "so the Wicket will have seen the Hummer leave and will think we're gone for the night."

"She has to believe no one is home," Zinnia said.

"Then we'll sneak back so we can watch all the fun," Rebecca said.

Which is exactly what we did.

It was too cloudy to see the moon that night, meaning it was very dark when nine bodies crept into our yard and hid behind a tree, one head peeking out over the other, so we could see it when the Wicket broke into our home for the second time in as many months.

Which wasn't hard to do, since we'd left the door unlocked for her.

We'd also left the front and back porch lights on so we could see things, since Marcia had checked the weather report and informed us there would be no moonlight.

Sometimes, we thought, Marcia was almost as smart as Annie.

We watched as the Wicket sneaked into our yard.

"Wow!" Will said in something quieter than a normal speaking voice but louder than a whisper. "The Wicket really does look like a toadstool!"

"Quiet!" Annie hushed him as the Wicket's head whipped around at the sound of noises in the dark.

Nine bodies held their breath, waiting to see what the Wicket would do next. Would she investigate? Would she just run away?

But no. After hearing no more peeps out of us, she entered our home, shutting the door behind her.

Nine bodies raced around to the back of the house

and peeked in the window of Mommy's private study.

So we were there to witness it when the Wicket entered the room. She didn't need to turn on the light; we'd left it on for her. We were there to witness it when she headed straight for Mommy's file cabinet. We were there to witness it when she looked through the top drawer until she found what she was looking for, all the way at the back, hidden behind the drawer itself: a folder that was marked *Nothing*.

We'll tell you, we were very surprised when, having opened the file, instead of removing the sheet of paper there, the Wicket whipped out a tiny thing and held it to her eye.

It took us a while to figure out what it was.

It was the kind of miniature camera a spy might use.

She was probably thinking that if she just took the sheet of paper, someone would notice it was missing and then try to track down the truth. But this way, she could take the information without leaving behind any evidence that she'd been there.

Who knew the Wicket could be so smart?

"Say," Will whispered, "you never said: what did you put in that folder?"

"It says . . . ," Annie started.

When she continued, her voice sounded as though she were looking at the letter herself, reading the words over the shoulder of the Wicket even as the Wicket was seeing them for the first time.

To Whom It May Concern:

Not safe here! Have taken
the secret of eternal life with
me and have escaped to China.
Don't look for me in Beijing!

Signed,

Lucy Huit

Annie was proud of how quickly she'd learned to forge Mommy's handwriting.

We looked back in the window just in time to see the expression of horror come over the Wicket's face as she actually read the sheet of paper she'd been so busily photographing.

We guessed that the Wicket hadn't planned on going all the way to the Far East to discover the secret of eternal life.

The Wicket did take the time to replace the *Nothing* folder back in its proper hiding place, behind the drawer. But then the house practically shook in its foundation as she pounded out of the room, leaving the lights on.

"Huh," Annie said. "Some people don't care about running other people's electricity all night when they don't have to pay the bills."

"Where is she going so fast?" Petal wanted to know.

"Oh," Annie said, smiling in the dark, "I'm pretty sure she's going to China."

Then a new thought occurred to her.

"Gee," she said, "I hope she doesn't call Social Services before she jets off the Beijing, to tell them our mother isn't living here anymore."

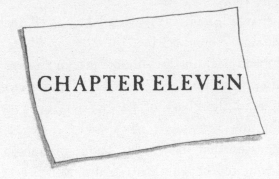

CHAPTER ELEVEN

But we didn't think she'd taken the time to do that.

How could she have?

Within the hour, we saw a cab pull up in front of her little house. Then we watched as the Wicket, holding a suitcase tied together with string, hopped into the back seat.

When the cab had pulled safely around the corner, we snuck over into the Wicket's yard and saw that she'd nailed boards crookedly all over the front door, sealing it shut.

"Oh, she's off to Beijing all right," Annie said as we strolled back into our own yard.

"Yea!" Petal said once we were back in our own home. "The Wicket is gone!"

"Yea!" Zinnia said. "Let's celebrate!"

"We should go to the beach!" Durinda suggested.

"The beach?" Will looked at us, surprised. "In the middle of winter?"

So we took Will on a tour of all of our seasonal rooms, ending the tour in Summer.

Summer had a sandy floor with shovels and pails and beach umbrellas and sunlamps. It was the perfect place to go for a celebration since, it still being February, we were all sick of winter.

"This is fantastic!" Will said, his face turned up to catch the light of one of the sunlamps. "I'm pretty sure I'm getting a tan!"

While Will sunned his handsome face, the rest of us kicked off our shoes, removed our socks, and played a rousing game of beach volleyball.

"This is fun!" Petal shouted.

"Hit it to me!" Zinnia shouted.

"Do you think you could not kick sand in my face?" Rebecca said to Georgia. "Or step on my toes?"

"Ouch!" Durinda shouted.

Ouch?

"Are you okay?" Jackie asked as Durinda hopped around on one foot, holding the other in her hands.

"What's wrong with Durinda?" Marcia wanted to know.

"I swear I didn't step on her feet," Georgia said.

"No, of course you didn't!" Durinda said. She was obviously angry, and we all took a step away from her, worried that in her anger she might freeze us where we stood. We were too busy having fun to be frozen just then.

"I stepped on something with my toe!" Durinda said. "And it hurts!"

Usually, Durinda, who tended to be the mommy among us since Mommy disappeared, took care of the rest of us. But now it was our turn to take care of her.

"Let me see," Annie said as we approached Durinda with care. We were using care because we still worried Durinda might freeze us.

Then Annie sat Durinda down in the nearest beach chair and looked at the bottom of her foot.

In Durinda's big toe, there was a tiny prick, not much bigger than what a pin might make.

"Huh," Annie said, "I wonder what caused that."

"It's so odd," Jackie said. "Daddy was always so careful to make sure Mommy didn't leave anything that could be dangerous in the seasonal rooms."

"It's true," Rebecca said, a rare sad look on her face. "Daddy was always so good at looking out for us."

But we didn't have time to be any sadder than that just then, because Dandruff had heard her mistress's howl and entered the room to investigate.

Zinnia, being crazy little Zinnia, bent to whisper something in Dandruff's ear and pointed with her little finger to where Durinda had been standing when she'd been injured.

Then Dandruff hurriedly padded over to the spot and began churning up sand with her paws.

Her ears pricked up after just a short few seconds of churning. Then she bent her head and opened her mouth, as though she were about to eat something, then closed her mouth again.

Dandruff padded back to Durinda and brushed her furry head against Durinda's hand until she opened her palm. Then Dandruff dropped something green and glittery in that open palm.

It was a dangly earring, the gemstone of which was the color of an emerald.

We looked at it in fascination.

Green, as we all knew, was Durinda's favorite color. It had always seemed a strange favorite color for a person to have, but that was Durinda all over.

We looked at the earring more closely.

It was one of those old-fashioned ones that clipped on with a tiny screw, which was a good thing since none of us had our ears pierced.

"How odd," Durinda said. "Who would wear just one earring? It's not like I'm a pirate or something."

Zinnia bent down next to Dandruff again, only this time we could hear what she whispered.

"Do you think you might find another one of these?" Zinnia asked.

Of course, we knew the cat couldn't understand her, but it was still wonderful when Dandruff went back to the same spot, churning up beach sand like crazy until she was able to return proudly with the second earring, dropping it in Durinda's outstretched hand.

Durinda slowly screwed the earrings on.

"How do I look?" she asked.

"Like a princess," Petal said.

"Like someone who was lucky enough to find her gift." Zinnia sighed.

"Say!" Jackie said, excitement in her eyes. "We should go to the drawing room to see if there's a new note behind that loose stone in the wall!"

"Note?" Will wondered.

We'd told him about the first note, the one about what we'd need to do to discover what happened to our parents, but we'd never explained about the notes that had been coming ever since.

But there was no time to explain now as we raced through the house and into the drawing room, Will in hot pursuit.

It was Annie who removed the loose stone from the wall.

"There is definitely a new note in there," she announced. But then she stepped away from the stone and gestured for Durinda to step forward. "I'm pretty sure," Annie said, "this one's for you."

We all looked over Durinda's shoulder as she read her note:

Dear Durinda,

Again, nice work. The Eights are doing just great: four down, twelve to go.

As always, the note was unsigned.

We still wanted to know who was putting them there.

"There are those great math skills again," Marcia observed.

"I *love* this house!" Will shouted.

CHAPTER TWELVE

"You know," Annie began after Will had departed.

When Will's mother had arrived to pick him up, we told Mrs. Simms that our parents were too busy watching TV to come to the door, but they were really happy she had let Will come for a visit. They hoped he would come back often.

"You know," Annie said again as we all sat around the drawing room, "just because the Wicket is out of the way, off on her wild-goose chase to China, it doesn't mean we're out of the woods yet."

"How do you mean?" Jackie asked.

"It's simply this," Annie said. "The Wicket might not be our only enemy. Think about it."

We thought about it.

We'd been so relieved to have the Wicket finally gone, we hadn't thought beyond that.

But we did now.

Our parents were still missing, or dead, and there could still be other enemies at large.

There could be a lot of enemies.

There was so much we still had to accomplish, so much we still didn't know.

"Not only that," Annie said after she'd given us a lot of time to think, "but just because the Wicket is off in China now, it doesn't mean she'll necessarily remain there forever."

"How do you mean?" Jackie asked again.

"Think about it," Annie said again.

So we did.

First we pictured the Wicket arriving in China and locating Beijing—wherever that was. She'd turn the entire city inside out, looking for Mommy and her secret to eternal life. Then, not finding Mommy or the secret, she'd realize she'd been tricked and she'd return home . . .

Angry.

The idea of an angry Wicket was too awful to think about, so we stopped.

And it was easy to stop because just then Durinda said, "Let's not think about that now. Let's break out the frozen pizza and cans of pink frosting and think about all the good things that have happened instead."

So that's what we did.

* * * * * * * *

"Yes, let's think about the good things," Durinda said after she'd used her power to freeze Rebecca before she could snag the last slice of pizza and then had waited for her to unfreeze again. "We've done so much these last two months."

"Why, just this month alone look what we've done!" Annie said.

"We discovered our mother was—*is*—a genius," Durinda said.

"We got rid of the Wicket," Georgia said.

"At least for now," Jackie added.

"We solved our little refrigeration problem," Marcia said.

"As well as the romantic problems of Carl the talking refrigerator and robot Betty," Petal said.

"With a little help from Pete," Rebecca corrected.

"Ah, Pete." Zinnia sighed. "I wish we could have gone to live with the Petes."

We all sighed as we thought of what that would have been like, but we did understand it wasn't possible.

"At least we made Mandy feel good with the card we gave her," Zinnia said. "It's always nice for people to get things."

"And at least," Jackie said, "we finally confided in Will about what's been going on here."

We all sighed, thinking of Will.

It had been so nice having him there.

But in a way, it was nice just being us again.

"I found my power and gift in January," Annie said.

"And I found mine in February," Durinda said.

"Say," Marcia said, light dawning in her eyes, "does anyone else see a pattern forming here?"

"How do you mean?" Annie asked.

Annie looked a bit angry. We thought it probably bothered Annie when one of us figured out something smart about something before she did. We also thought it was probably a good thing that Annie didn't have Durinda's power to freeze Marcia where she sat.

"Well," Marcia said, "we'd already agreed that there was one pattern: we Eights are getting our powers and gifts in order of when we were born. Right?"

Seven heads nodded.

"But it could also be alphabetical order," Rebecca said.

"Same difference," Marcia said.

"It doesn't have to go on that way, though," Zinnia pointed out. "Just because it's been that way so far, it doesn't mean it won't change."

Poor Zinnia. She was still upset by the idea of always being last and was hoping for a reprieve. But of course she was wrong. Of course it wouldn't change.

"But here's a second pattern," Marcia announced. "As Annie says, she got her power and gift in January, now Durinda has gotten hers in February—"

"That means we each get our own month!" Jackie cried, cutting her off. "Each of us Eights gets her very own month in which she'll find her own power and gift!"

"Hmm," Georgia said, "I wonder which one of us will be next . . ."

We all looked at Georgia. The idea of Georgia getting her turn in March seemed like it could be a scary one. Spring suddenly seemed too close and March too soon.

"Then I really will be last!" Zinnia cried, only her cry wasn't a happy one like Jackie's had been. It was a sad cry, complete with a tear. "In order to get my day in the sun, I'll have to wait until stinking August!"

"There, there." Annie put her arm around Zinnia's shoulders.

"But it isn't fair!" Zinnia cried.

"What in our lives is?" Annie said gently. "And, anyway, haven't you ever heard about saving the best for last?"

Zinnia's tears dried like dew on the grass that's been kissed by the sun.

"Do you mean it?" Zinnia asked. "You really believe that?"

"Oh, yes," Annie said, proving she was still our smart girl. "And your month, I just have a feeling, is going to be a doozy."

Zinnia smiled so bright then, even if it hadn't still been night, even if it were daytime and the sun hung in the sky, that sun could never have been as bright as Zinnia's smile.

Then we crowded around Zinnia, all hugging one another so close we were like a giant sunflower; it was impossible to tell where one girl ended and the next began or who was hugging whom.

"And so," Durinda said, and that's when we realized she was at our center, at least for now, "our story continues . . ."